Bre

When Eme on horseback she knew immediately who it was. He wasn't sixteen any longer, but she needed no one to tell her it was the viscount. He was even more handsome than she had remembered; very sophisticated now. There was knowledge in the eyes which met hers . . .

Nicholas was transfixed. She was breathtaking from the top of her glossy hair to the tips of her shoes. She had filled out slightly, but not too much. Time had rounded her breasts and hips delightfully, but he could have spanned her tiny waist with his hands.

They went on gazing at each other. . . Emerald felt exactly the same sensation as she had done on the first occasion she had seen him. It was like making love again. A sensual, passionate, exciting union, as if they were naked in bed . . .

It was the same for Asterly and he felt the chill of defeat on him.

She remained the girl of his fantasies and he still loved her with the same terrible, destructive force.

EMERALD

Helen Ashfield

St. Martin's Press
New York

EMERALD

Copyright © 1983 by Helen Ashfield

Printed in the United States of America

First St. Martin's Press mass market edition/July 1986

ISBN: 0-312-90173-9

10 9 8 7 6 5 4 3 2 1

Acknowledgements

I am deeply grateful to the following authors whose informative and wholly fascinating works enabled me to write this novel:

Shops and Shopping: 1800-1914, Alison Adburgham
Bond Street, Ivor Halstead
Shopping in Style, Alison Adburgham
Life in Victorian London, L.C.B. Seaman
The Age of Worth, Edith Saunders
A History of Regent Street, Hermione Hobhouse
A History of Shopping, Dorothy Davis
The Story of Cornwall, A.K. Hamilton Jenkin
A Victorian Village, Mary French
Cornish Villages, Donald R. Rawe
Cornwall, Robin Davidson
Vanishing Cornwall, Daphne du Maurier
Harbour Village: Yesterday in Cornwall, Leon Tregenza
Early Tide: A Mevagissey Childhood, Mary Lakeman
Human Documents of the Victorian Golden Age, W Royston Pike
Kings of Fashion, Anny Latour
The Workwoman's Guide by "A Lady"
Strata of Society: Costume Society Conference. The Dressmaker's Craft, Various contributors
The Tailoring and Dressmaking Trades 1700-1850, Madeleine Ginsburg
The Perfect Lady, C. Willett Cunnington

Emerald

Handbook of English Costume – 19C, C. Willett Cunnington and Phillis Cunnington
The Fashionable Lady in the 19C, Charles H. Gibbs-Smith
V & A 19th Century Costume, Introduction by James Laver
Elegant Modes in the Nineteenth Century, Angus Holden
Portrait of Polperro, Sheila de Burlet

H A.

ONE
Cornwall; 1830

At the ripe old age of ten years and three months, Emily Tregellan sat at the breakfast table and made a thorough and unchildlike assessment of her situation.

It was six-thirty on a stormy morning late in March. The weather had been vicious for the past few weeks and the fishermen of Porthaven were in despair. It was as if the raging sea had become a monster which had devoured all the fish itself, leaving the waters empty and hostile.

Some families had a store of salted pilchards left; many did not. Women begged for credit at the local shop and prayed that the gale might catch a ship between savage tentacles and dash it against the rocks. Then there would be rich pickings to be had. Barrels of bacon, butter, tea, flour and brandy would be washed up on the shore and everyone would have their fill. So far, the Almighty had ignored the entreaties and most continued to go hungry.

Emily had eaten her mouthful of barley bread, washed down with half a mug of milk, watered to make it go further. It had whetted her appetite rather than assuaging it, but there was no more to be had.

To distract her mind from her rumbling stomach, Emily let her gaze wander round the crowded living-room and then over her family. Her brothers, Jude, Matthew and Saul, merited no more than a second's attention. They were rough, noisy and forever teasing her. She spat her resentment at them when they called her a ninny for washing her hair so often in rain-water from the butt outside, but that merely egged them on to greater insults.

Hilda, a two-year-old tyrant, was screaming for more milk but she was also dismissed.

Emily's eyes came to rest on her father. Morris Tregellan was a fisherman, like his father and grandfather before him. Somehow they had been able to cope with their problems; Morris could not.

His lugger was old and near the end of its life. When the fish returned, there was no guarantee that *The Lucy Rose* would be of any use, even for inshore fishing. Calamity stared at him without compassion. Morris lived in a world where only the strong survived.

He claimed that he was dogged by ill-luck and that the evils which beset him were not of his own making. Emily had heard the villagers deny this most emphatically, calling him a weak fool who'd got just what he deserved.

They were no more charitable as far as her mother, Ancilla, was concerned. She was a scraggy creature, prematurely old, and filled with self-pity. She was complaining now of sickness, for she was with child again. She and Morris had seven children whom they couldn't feed or cloth, yet another demanding mouth was on its way.

Large families were commonplace, but the women gossiping outside the shop which sold everything from rope to ribbon were trenchant in their criticism.

"She ought to send that husband of hers about his business," one had said. "Seven of 'em now and everyone as thin as a pole and half of 'em as sick as a shag."

They hadn't known Emily was in earshot, but it was doubtful if they would have stilled their tongues, even if they had been aware of her presence.

"Never mended a net in her life. Useless, that's what she is."

Mrs Polglase, more kindly disposed than the rest, had pointed out that Ancilla had been born with a deformed left hand and that the hard task of repairing the nets would have been too much for her. She had been put in her place at once.

"She could try, if she'd a mind for it," had been the tart response. "Never cooks neither, not that she's got much for the pot. I'd be shamed to let my eldest do it while I sat on my bottom and watched."

There had been a chorus of agreement. There was never enough to eat, but whatever came to hand was prepared with loving care, each woman proud of her culinary skills.

"And that cottage of hers," a third had chimed in. "Fair turned my stomach the day I called to offer a mite of cheese to help out, as it were. Why, I wouldn't put our sow in a place like that."

The women's words faded from Emily's consciousness, but the truth of what they had said wasn't so easy to forget.

Externally, the Tregellan's cottage was like most others in the village. There was a fish-cellar at ground level, living accommodation above. The latter was reached by a flight of worn stone steps, rising from the narrow alley which coiled like a snake between the rows of houses.

Emily had seen inside the cottages of one or two of their neighbours. Upon being invited to 'take a peep at my parlour, why don't you?' she had been torn between amazement and mortification. She had stared at the well-scrubbed tables, carefully dusted chairs, the rag-rugs on the floors, and dressers filled with bright china. Some had even got a picture or two on the walls and one had a pot of flowers in the window.

Emily's home was very different. There was only one chair and that had been appropriated by her mother. Her father sat on a stool, the children on odd lumps of wood brought up from the beach. Wet clothes hung on lines stretched across the ceiling; dust and grease covered the floor and rickety table.

That morning Emily seemed to see everything with a new and dissecting eye. It was a very special day for her, for she was to become a wage-earner like her brothers who helped the carpenter and the sail-maker for a copper or two.

From eight o'clock in the morning until five in the

afternoon Emily was to assist Miss Oonagh Pezzach, the dressmaker who lived in the village and churchtown of Paul, right up on the hill above Porthaven. She would pick up pins and cottons, thread needles, sweep up cuttings and generally make herself useful. When she left the seamstress she was to go to the Trefusis farm, half a mile away, there to labour on until seven.

"Might as well make a day of it," her father had said when he had informed Emily of her future. "Sixpence a week from Miss Pezzach and tuppence from Mrs Trefusis. Time you started to earn your keep."

Emily had almost laughed in her father's face, but she knew better than to rile him. His horny hand was always quick to mete out punishment, particularly where she was concerned. She was regarded as the rebel of the family, sharp with her tongue and far too conceited about her appearance. They couldn't think why she wrapped herself in a piece of sacking so often, simply in order to wash and darn her only dress. She knew they never would understand. Dirt didn't bother them as it bothered her.

She wrinkled her nose in disgust as the stench from the earthenware lamp reached her nostrils. The oil it burnt came from pilchards and the smell clung to clothes and skin if one was foolish enough to get too near to the light.

"If you've finished eating, best be on your way, Emily." Morris was sucking on an empty pipe, craving for a pinch of tobacco. "Won't do for you to be late first morning."

"Not much past seven, Pa."

"Maybe not, still it's a fair walk up the hill and there's no point in you idling here."

Emily contained her frustration. Her mother spent her whole time in idleness, watching her children struggle with the jobs she should have been doing. She grumbled at Jess as the latter kneaded dough and placed it on the stone in the open hearth, covering it with a pot and drawing hot ashes over it. She scolded as the girl tried to make a thin soup in the cauldron hanging over the fire, using a few potatoes, a turnip and a meat bone, when she could get one. When Jess cooked hoggan, a lump of dough with a fragment of bacon in the centre, Ancilla was swift to point out how much better she had done it when she was on her feet.

And whilst Ancilla fed her latest infant, or held her distended belly filled with yet another Tregellan, Emily tried to scour the table, wash the floor and stop the younger ones from eating mouthfuls of the peat which was kept in a box on one side of the chimney recess.

Their efforts were rewarded by nagging from their mother and a cuff from their father if they got in his way. If caught out in a moment of slackness the penalty was worse than a blow. That meant bed, without a scrap of supper, lying on bare boards trying to forget the pangs of hunger.

Emily wiped the resentment from her eyes. This was the beginning of a new life for her and she didn't want it to start with a belting from her father.

"All right, Pa."

She rose and nodded to her mother. No one ever exchanged a kiss in that household and seldom a smile. There was neither love nor affection; just indifference, toil, and the common effort of clinging to the precarious existence which they shared.

"Suppose your hands are clean?" Ancilla put a fist in the small of her back and groaned. Another week, perhaps two, and she would be nursing a new offspring. She didn't want the child, but Morris was not a man to be refused, selfish to the core as he demanded his rights. "You're forever washing them, you stuck-up little madam, but let me see. "Don't want that prissy old maid saying my gels are dirty."

Emily didn't answer, simply holding out her hands for inspection. They were spotless, each nail pink and shiny. When all her jobs were done, Emily would rub away at her nails until they gleamed. It wasn't that she was conceited as her mother thought; she just considered her body was worth caring for.

"You'll do, I suppose." Ancilla was grudging. "All right for you to go off like this, but it leaves everything to Jess. I'm in no fit state to help."

It was on the tip of Emily's tongue to remind her mother that she would be glad enough of the wages, come Saturday, but she knew her father was watching her.

"Well, go on then." Ancilla waved her away. "Like your pa says, no sense in hanging around here."

"See you keep a civil tongue in your head," warned Tregellan, his teeth grinding on the stem of the pipe. Other men seemed to find a ha'penny to buy baccy, but he never could. "Don't want you losing this job through your sauciness."

"I'll remember." Suddenly Emily was anxious to be gone. "I'll do what you say."

Jess followed Emily outside, a small package in her hand. If Emily had any feelings at all for her kin they were reserved for her elder sister. She felt scorn for her when she cringed away from their father like a beaten dog, but Jess was never spiteful and always willing to take on extra work when Emily's eyelids began to droop.

"Don't know as Miss Pezzach'll give you a bite come dinner-time," she whispered. "There's a bit of bread in here and a cold potato. Not much, I know, but it's all there is."

Emily felt an unexpected lump in her throat.

"What'll you have?"

"I'll find something."

"If I get anything I'll bring this back for your supper, I promise."

"Don't matter. I'm too tired to eat most nights."

Emily took a closer look at her sister's face. Fourteen and looking nearer thirty. Fatigue had robbed Jess's cheeks of their colour, drained her eyes and left her lips as pale as whey.

"I'm going to get away from here, soon as I can," said Emily, her scrutiny done. "I'll not stay and grow like Ma.

There's got to be more to life than that and I'm going to find it, no matter what I have to do."

"Don't let Pa hear you talk like that."

"I won't."

"Perhaps you'll marry one day." Jess worried about Emily, sensing there was something different about her without understanding what it was. "Hope you do, anyway."

"I'll not marry a man from round here."

"Porthaven girls always marry Porthaven men. You know that."

"I shan't." Emily was firm. "I won't wed a penniless fisherman who'll put me in the family way every year."

"Emily Tregellan! What a thing to say, and at your age too."

"Mrs Treve said it only the other day." Emily was unrepentant. "She was talking about Ma."

"Be that as it may, you've no cause to repeat it."

"All right, but I'm still not going to stay here. I'm going to be rich and famous one day."

Jess relaxed. It was just Em's daydreams again.

"That's silly talk. I said you were a child. You'll grow out of your fancies soon enough."

"No, I won't. Silly or not, I'm going to make it happen. You'd better go in now; ma's calling you."

"Take care, mind. Hope Miss Pezzach's a good un."

"So do I, but if she ain't I won't be worse off than at home."

Emily turned away, pretending not to notice the moisture in her sister's eyes. It was no use weakening, whatever lay ahead. That, at least, was a lesson Morris had taught his daughter well. She looked back once to wave to Jess and then began to trudge up the steep slope. Yesterday lay behind her; today and tomorrow beckoned her on and she wasn't going to refuse the invitation.

"It's starting," she cried and lifted her arms to the heavens as if she had just been let out of a cage. "Now I'm going to begin again and this time I'll make it better or my name's not Emily Tregellan. This time I'm going to get it right."

When she reached the top of the headland Emily paused. The clouds were still ominous and the wind bit like a knife. Below her the churning sea was rushing into the harbour, striking the far pier and shooting upwards in a column of white spray which seemed to hang in the air for ever. It was wonderful to watch and she never tired of the spectacle, even though such storms meant no catch and thus no supper.

Further along the cliff top was a place from which one could look down on the whole village. Whenever Emily had a free hour, which wasn't very often, she would take the path up to her favourite spot, lying flat on her stomach as she forgot reality and gave her imagination free rein.

From that distance Porthaven looked so small. The tiny houses of granite or stone seemed to creep up the base of the hill in tiers, some red-topped, others with roofs of Delabole slate. Then they stopped, giving way to the high ground above, knowing they couldn't fight the elements up there.

The boats were mere dots, tossed back and forth at anchor; the sea wall was draped with nets, black and tangled like the hair of a witch.

In her make-believe world there were no fishermen, stonemasons, carpenters or men labouring in the barking-houses where the nets were cleaned and cured. Emily peopled her fantasy village with grand ladies and gentlemen, although she herself had never seen such important personages. She knew they existed though, because some of the women had daughters in service. When the girls came home on a visit they were full of the goings-on of their employers, talking endlessly of a way of life which Emily couldn't begin to envisage.

No one seemed to mind when she listened open-mouthed to the tales of banquets and balls and painted women in silks and satins with jewels in their tresses. It was difficult to picture what such materials were like, or what was meant by imbecile sleeves and pelerines, but Emily drank in every word, storing them all in her memory, for she knew they were important. When the mothers got tired of their daughters' stories, chiding them for shewing off and belittling their own folk, the girls were glad enough to turn to Emily. They knew she would accept with near reverence their knowledge of *manches a gigot*, boned corsets, bustles and Leghorn hats.

"I'll have a gown of printed muslin one day," said Emily aloud, her voice swept away by the screech of the storm. "A pelerine too, whatever that is, made of finest lace and a hat with flowers and feathers on it."

Suddenly she became aware of time, scrambling to her feet and running the rest of the way to Paul, the village named after St Pol de Leon. Now that the moment was nearly upon her, Emily felt a twinge of nervousness about the job into which her father had forced her. She was thankful to get away from her mother's querulous demands, Daisy's whining and Hilda, who was forever wetting the floor. But for once she had doubts about herself and her ability to please Miss Pezzach. She had no skills to offer and, as Jess had reminded her, she was still only a child. If the seamstress was a tartar, she'd soon tire of Emily's uselessness and send her packing.

However, there was no turning back and Emily slowed down as she made her way past the church and inn to Miss Pezzach's doorstep.

Oonagh Pezzach was fifty-two, slight of build, with neatly dressed hair and a gown of blue wool trimmed with braid. She had only lived in Paul for ten years and was still regarded as something of a stranger. People nodded at her quite politely and she had sufficient clients to keep her going, but she was an outsider and she knew it.

She opened the door and looked down at Emily, utterly spellbound and conscious of two inescapable truths. The first was that Tregellan's daughter was the loveliest human being she had ever seen. Her skin was as pure as alabaster, the bone structure of her face like a precious work of art. Dark silky hair reached down to her waist; her eyes were brilliant emeralds, full of enquiry.

The second thing which struck Miss Pezzach was the fact that Emily was a fighter. It showed in the jut of her small chin and the steadfast line of her mouth. Emily wasn't going to let her hard life get her down. She was going to stand up to fate's knocks and do some hitting back of her own.

It was in that first moment of their meeting that Oonagh Pezzach began to respect Emily, certain beyond doubt that she would never have cause to change her judgement.

"Come in, Emily; you're soaked."

Miss Pezzach didn't ask why she wasn't wearing a cloak, for she already knew. Fisherfolk couldn't afford such things. A skimpy dress clung to the slender body and it wasn't difficult to see that a wrap was not the only thing which was lacking. Oonagh was a very sensitive woman and she had read pride in Emily, too. She would have to tread very cautiously.

"I fear you'll take a chill unless we can get you into something warm," she said in a very matter-of-fact tone. "It so happens that I've got a gown upstairs about your size. It was an order, but it was never collected. Some people are so thoughtless; I'd put a lot of work into it. Would you object to wearing it so it doesn't go to waste?"

Emily considered Miss Pezzach in silence, the latter well aware that she was on trial. Then she was rewarded with a nod which made her ridiculously happy. Emily had understood and didn't mind the offer.

Oonagh poured hot water into a tin bath in her bedroom, lighting the fire and putting towels in front of it to warm, explaining anxiously that this was the best way to avoid a bad cold. Emily agreed, seeing the genuine concern in her employer. It wasn't charity; it was common sense. For a ten-year-old, Emily was very practical.

The steaming water was a luxury, the scented soap a new and incredible experience. Tactfully, Oonagh had left the room after pointing out the gown, a shift and three petticoats which lay on the bed.

Later, clad in lilac-coloured merino and a pair of Miss Pezzach's stockings, Emily sipped tea, which she had never tasted before. She tried not to gobble up the generous slice of fruit cake served on a plate made of eggshell china, but it wasn't easy.

"I'll be very careful not to get a mark on it." Emily stroked the folds of the skirts with a butterfly touch. She wanted to hold it against her cheek so she could feel its sensuous warmth, but Miss Pezzach would think her soft in the head if she did that. "I'm reel grateful."

Oonagh felt tears very near. Emily was so young, yet she spoke like an adult. Grinding poverty left no loopholes for the natural ways of childhood.

"You're welcome," she said casually. "As a matter of a fact, I've really no use for it and the moths might get at it if it's left in the cupboard. Why don't you keep it?"

Emily grew very quiet and Mizz Pezzach cursed her own folly. She had so wanted to get to know this girl better; even to make a friend of her. But she had moved too quickly. Now Emily was offended and would probably run off with a mumbled excuse.

When she found her fears had no substances, it was as if a great weight had been lifted from her heart.

"I'd like that, but I can only wear it when I'm here. It wouldn't last five minutes at home. Our cottage isn't like this, you see, and I've got the floor to scrub and the sty to muck out. I couldn't bear to spoil the dress. Besides, it might make Jess miserable because she hadn't got one too."

"Your sister?"

"Yes. Can't exactly say I love her, but she's better than the rest. She gave me a bit of bread and potato to bring with me for my dinner. It were hers, but she let me have it."

Miss Pezzach blew her nose hastily. She had never met anyone quite like Emily before.

"I see. I had hoped you'd share my meal at midday. I've had a casserole on since first thing. You do like casserole, don't you?"

"Not sure what it is, but I thank you kindly for the offer. Now I can take the bread and potato back with me so Jess can have it for her supper."

Oonagh wanted to rush to her larder and raid it for butter, flour, eggs, sugar and meat, pressing the food upon Emily, but she realised that that would shatter the fragile relationship between them. She would have to be patient yet, even as she accepted that, part of her mind was planning the following day's meal – something hot, tasty and plenty of it.

"Very well," she said when she was sure her voice wouldn't give her away. "Just wear the dress when you're here, but no one would notice if you kept one of the petticoats, would they? It would help to keep you warm."

"No, don't suppose they would."

"Good, then that's settled. Now, my dear, if you've finished your tea let me show you what I want you to do."

She paused, aware of Emily's earnest concentration.

"I can't tell you how glad I'll be to have you here. I get very depressed by myself. Loneliness is a terrible thing."

"So is unloneliness."

The dressmaker frowned.

"Unloneliness? I don't think I understand."

"It's wanting to be by yourself and not being able to. To have so many others round you all the time, talking, shouting, crying, quarrelling and smelling till you can't think proper."

Oonagh felt her heart quicken again. She had been right about Emily. There was something very special about the child who was trying so hard to please.

"Ah, yes. I hadn't thought about that, but I do see what you mean. Perhaps we'll be good for one another and I promise not to shout."

"And I'll promise to stop you feeling sad." The red lips parted in a wide, friendly smile. "Oh, Miss Pezzach; I'm ever so glad to be here."

The moment Emily saw Miss Pezzach's workroom she knew what her life was going to be.

Intended as a dining-room, it had been cleared of all furniture save two long tables and a chair or two. On one table was the gown Oonagh was making, a striped confection with fashionable sleeves the size of balloons, the wide hem of the skirt stiffened with 'crin'.

The other table was piled high with lengths of velvet, satin, levantine, taffeta, organdie and gingham, side by side with baskets of ribbons, braid, buttons and a froth of lace.

Emily moved forward like one in a dream. She had never expected to see the gorgeous materials which she'd heard about so often, but there they were before her in all their glory. Pinks and shot-blues, yellows and greens, stripes and checks and flowered muslins of every hue.

Miss Pezzach watched her face, sensing that something very important was happening. She knew she was being foolish. It was only the natural reaction of a humble village girl to the trappings of the wealthy which she had never seen before. Yet she couldn't shake off the feeling that she was witnessing an event, the memory of which would remain with her for the rest of her days.

"Emily?"

Finally Emily turned to Oonagh as the real world rushed back.

"This is what I'm going to do too," she said breathlessly. "I wasn't sure until this moment, but now I am. I know I'm only here to pick up pins for you, but one day I'm going to be a dressmaker too. But I'll be ..."

She broke off in confusion.

"You'll be what, dear?"

"I can't say."

"You'll be successful, is that it?"

Emily hung her head.

"I didn't mean it like it sounded."

"I know. Don't concern yourself. Perhaps one day you will achieve your goal but you must understand how many years it takes, even to be like me."

Emily blushed again.

"I'm ever so sorry I said that; I could bite my tongue out. But I wouldn't care how long it took, just so I got there in the end. I'm too young to start learning yet, I suppose."

"Not necessarily. I know of a charity school where girls of ten have been taught to cut out from patterns and sew a very creditable seam. It's hard work, you know."

"I wouldn't mind that."

"Well, we'll see how you get on with picking up pins, shall we? The first thing I want you to do is to keep the workbox tidy. It contains all the tools of my trade and I never allow it to get in a muddle. See, here it is."

Oonagh opened the lid of a mahogany box divided into sections and Emily drew closer, fascinated by the orderly array of reels of cotton, yarn and silk; tapes; hooks and eyes; needles and pins, and a pair of tweezers.

"These are the scissors." Miss Pezzach unwrapped six pairs from the soft piece of leather protecting them. "Each one is right for a particular job and they have to be kept sharp and free from rust."

"What are those pictures, Miss Oonagh?"

"Fashion-plates from Paris. One of my customers has left them with me, for she wants three gowns copied from them."

"Three! She must be very rich."

"Some ladies order six at a time, so we're going to be very busy. Now we must get started, for Mrs Pender wants that dress over there first thing tomorrow. Will you thread some needles for me, please? That size, and use the reel of light blue cotton."

"Yes, Miss Oonagh. When I've done that, may I watch you?"

"Of course, but make sure you keep my needles coming, won't you? I do hope you won't get bored."

She stole a glance at Emily's face, the odd feeling stronger than ever. She was quite certain her assistant wouldn't tire of what she was doing, but she wanted to hear the girl say it in words.

"I shan't." Emily's eyes met Oonagh's, almost steely in their resolution. "How can you get tired of your future? Here's the first needle and the second's ready too. Shall we begin?"

A month later Miss Pezzach experienced a small miracle which confirmed her feelings about Emily. She had grown fond of her in the four weeks they had spent together. Emily was very deft of hand, her mind quick and intuitive. Whatever Oonagh asked for, it was passed to her before she had finished speaking, and Emily never had to be shewn anything twice.

At first she was bothered that Emily had to go to the Trefusis farm after a long day with her, but it was clear that Emily was taking it all in her stride. When she chatted over the midday meal, Oonagh was told all about Mrs Trefusis's baking and the wonder of the farmhouse kitchen.

One afternoon, when the last garment had been laid aside, Oonagh went to make a cup of tea as she always did before Emily left. She cut bread and butter, spooned some jam into a glass dish, and added a piece of plum cake. In spite of Mrs Trefusis's cooking, Emily was always hungry.

When she got back to the workroom she found Emily's head bent over a scrap of red satin, her small thumb and finger flattening the material as swiftly she slipped her needle in and out of the hem.

"May I see that?"

Emily jumped, for she had quite forgotten her

surroundings.

"Miss Oonagh, I'm sorry. I didn't mean to steal this. I thought it wasn't wanted."

"It isn't and don't look like that. I'm not scolding you. I just want to see what you've done."

Emily rose quickly, rubbing one foot against the other as she waited for the verdict. It seemed to her that Miss Pezzach was going to stare at the bit of satin for ever, but finally the dressmaker looked up.

"Emily, could you take these two pieces of taffeta and sew and fell them? You've seen me do it, haven't you? Now you try."

Emily was in some trepidation because Miss Pezzach hadn't passed judgment on the hemming, but she wasted no time in selecting the right needle and yarn.

When it was finished Emily gave it to Miss Pezzach, not daring to speak. Oonagh gave a sigh. It hadn't been a fluke after all. The hem had been as near-perfect as any she'd seen; the felling was the same. The tiny stitches were almost invisible, exactly the same size, spaced with great precision. What was more, the material shewed no sign of having been handled and she looked up and smiled at Emily.

"You are very gifted, my dear. Of course, you've got a long road ahead, as I told you the first day we met, but it's all here. All you need is advanced tuition."

"Like in one of those places in London you told me about? Where all the girls sit in the back room together?"

"That's one way of learning, certainly."

"Tell me more about it."

"I've told you already, time and time again."

"Just once more – please!"

"All right, but drink your tea, for you'll have to be off soon. Well, I became an apprentice at the age of fourteen. I was lucky, for my parents were able to afford a premium of forty pounds so that I could go into one of the better fashion houses."

"Forty pounds is a fortune."

Oonagh chuckled.

"Yes, and all I got from the spending of it was two years of hard grind. At the end of that time I was an improver. That lasted for another year and then I got a salary of eight pounds a year and was able to boast of myself as an assistant. The next step was becoming a second hand; then a first hand. Finally, I became a superintendent, but the pressure was too much during the season and my health broke down.

"Oh, Emily, it's not easy; it isn't easy at all. One has to live on the business premises, unless one takes the chance of being an outdoor worker, which is not a good thing to be at all. We used to have breakfast at a quarter to eight and work right through until nine o'clock at night, with just two pauses of thirty minutes for dinner and tea. In the season, as I said, it was quite terrible. Often we wouldn't stop until twelve o'clock at night, even later sometimes."

Emily, no stranger to hard work, nodded. She was unconcerned by the thought of such a long day, hoping Miss Pezzach would go on.

"Then there was the workroom." Oonagh pulled a face. "It was dreadfully hot, with no ventilation, and some of us were prone to fainting fits after ten hours or so in such an atmosphere. The customers were so demanding. They had no thought for the girls who slaved away behind the scenes. They ordered gowns at the last minute, expecting them to be finished in a day. Mostly they were, for trade was never turned away."

"I wouldn't mind the hours and I'd be glad to be warm."

"There are other risks, but you're too young for me to tell you about such things."

"Please! I've got to know everything. What risks? Do you mean you cut yourself with the scissors, or ...?

"No, no, much worse than that. When a girl is very poor, she sometimes takes steps to earn money in a reprehensible manner. If she doesn't, she starves. You see, if you went to

London, you would have to be an outdoor dressmaker, because your parents couldn't find the premium for you to live in. You would get about nine shillings a week and out of that you'd have to pay for lodgings, food, clothes and fuel, if you weren't to freeze to death. That's why the girls do it; they can't manage on such a pittance."

"Do what, Miss Oonagh?"

The seamstress looked more uncomfortable than ever.

"Well, they go out with gentlemen."

Emily thought about that for a while, her brows meeting in a frown.

"I don't see how that would help them buy food," she said finally, "nor put wood in the grate either, come to that."

"The men pay them for ...for services, my dear."

"Oh, I see." The puzzled look left Emily's face and she giggled. "You mean like Mary Keigwin, who obliges the farmer at Trevitha? Everyone in Porthaven says she's a bed-faggot, but she doesn't go short of anything. Is that what you meant?"

"Yes." Oonagh was taken aback by her precocious companion, but it was a great relief not to have to go into greater detail. "So, you see, there are many hazards in the capital."

"But what else can I do? How can I learn everything if I don't go to one of them places?"

"I could teach you," said Oonagh quietly. "I don't mean just showing you how to run and fell or stitch on braid. When I gave up my position, I knew nearly all there was to know about the trade. I even designed my own patterns and chose the colours to be used. I could pass on all my knowledge to you. It would take years, as I told you before; six or seven at least. However, at the end of it you'd be as proficient as any dressmaker in London, I can promise you that."

"But the money, Miss Oonagh. My pa ain't got forty pounds to give you."

Oonagh laughed.

"I don't want forty pounds; I just want to give you your future. Call it a kind of present, if you like. You have a rare skill, Emily, as these samples show. With that natural ability, perseverance, and patience, I can make you the famous dressmaker you want to be. Well, what do you say?"

"Oh, yes, please, Miss Oonagh. Oh, yes!"

"Then we'll start tomorrow. Your days of sweeping up bits of cotton and watching me are over. It's time you started real work and we'll begin with the basic stitches. You must have a firm foundation. The interesting things come later; much later. For a very long time it will be dull and back-breaking."

"It won't break my back," returned Emily stoutly, "and it won't be dull neither. I'll go on till I drop and one day, Miss Oonagh, I'll make you proud of me, I swears it."

Miss Pezzach looked into the shining eyes and smiled again.

"I believe you, Emily Tregellan, I believe you. One of these days I shall be very proud indeed to have known you.

TWO

Five years later, Emily Tregellan was a much better dressmaker than Oonagh Pezzach and the latter was the first to admit it.

Although her training was not completed, Emily's tremendous driving-force combined with an outstanding talent had brought her to the point where she could make any gown, however elaborate and difficult its construction.

Oonagh had developed rheumatism in her fingers and it had become increasingly difficult for her to sew, but no customer ever had to wait for a garment, nor had cause to complain about it. Emily saw to that.

Word had gone round the neighbourhood that Miss Pezzach's gowns were now the smartest in the West Country, but the resulting flood of orders left Emily totally unflustered. She could have four or five dresses on the go at the same time, moving gracefully along the table, putting a frill on here, adding a tuck or two there, snipping out tacking threads as she sang to herself.

Sometimes Oonagh found it difficult to believe that Emily was only just fifteen. When she was at work she wore her hair piled on top of her head, emphasizing the line of her long neck. The taffeta gown into which she changed hugged her small waist and hinted of the gentle budding of her breasts.

Things hadn't improved in the Tregellan ménage. Two more children had arrived since Emily had gone to Miss Pezzach's. Jess was like a shadow, coughing painfully day and night as her mother still sat in her chair and bemoaned her lot.

An old fisherman had given Morris another boat, but he hadn't known how to keep it in repair and it had become as unseaworthy as his original lugger. The lines scoring his forehead were deeper, his temper shorter

Although Emily gave her mother three shillings a week, she never let her family know the quality of her work. As far as they were concerned she was still doing a bit of plain sewing for Miss Oonagh which, according to Ancilla, was all she was fit for.

They didn't know either that Emily retained two shillings of her weekly wage, keeping it in what she called her 'Savings Bag' in Miss Pezzach's spare bedroom. One day, when she knew everything there was to know about her craft, she intended to go to London, but not penniless.

The day on which Emily fell in love was like any other. It was a hot July evening when she left the farm, slightly earlier than usual. She had on her old dress again and had let her hair down, looking younger as she skipped through the grass towards the uneven road beyond which were the high cliffs above Porthaven.

She saw the carriage ahead of her but took no particular notice of it. She'd seen it before, from a distance. It belonged to the Earl of Radfield, so Miss Pezzach had told her, as did Cloverley Park, the mansion where the earl lived with his wife and son, Viscount Asterly.

A flock of sheep halted the vehicle and Emily found herself beside it, watching as the shepherd tried to shoo his recalcitrant charges out of the nobleman's way. Then she glanced up and felt as if her heart had stopped beating.

Nicholas Roman, Viscount Asterly, was sixteen. He had brown hair curled round a well-shaped head beneath his tall Cumberland hat. The sun had turned his skin light bronze, but nature had bestowed even greater gifts. Clear eyes, as blue as the sea beyond the headland; a straight, proud nose; cheek and jaw bones which would still be beautiful when he was old.

He sensed someone there and turned quickly. He had never had an interest in girls before. Those he knew were silly and tiresome, patting their coiffeurs and flouncing about in the most absurd manner. He much preferred hunting or using the splendid pair of flintlock pistols with brass barrels and silver mounts which had been a present from a doting aunt.

The slender creature staring at him so intently was different. She looked wild and untamed. Strands of dark hair blew in the slight breeze and there was just a hint of pinkness in her cheeks which owed nothing to rouge. His mother, Juliet, had a necklace of emeralds, but they weren't as dazzling as the eyes which held his own.

She was a shock to him. He had never desired anyone before, but he wanted her. He knew he always would, although it was doubtful that they would ever see each other again. He didn't often ride that way and in any event he would be returning to Oxford before long.

Yet he wanted to stroke her white flesh with his fingers; encircle her waist with his arm; cup her breast with a tender hand so that he could feel the beat of her heart. Nicholas Roman had grown up in a matter of seconds.

The encounter was equally traumatic for Emily. For the first time in her life she was really conscious of her body. Hitherto it had simply been a thing to be cared for, kept as clean as circumstances permitted, fed and exercised to keep it healthy.

Now she was aware of it in quite a different way. She could feel it, as the handsome young man was seeing it, blushing because suddenly she realised her dress was too tight. The thin material strained across the bodice, outlining her bosom and pinpointing the nipples. The skirt was torn up to her left thigh and she tried to hide the smooth suppleness of her leg as she tugged at the ragged edges.

She knew he was drinking in every inch of her, as if he

were possessing her, but she didn't resent it. It was like
making love and her lips parted, wanting his mouth against
her own. She was roused as never before. Men to her had
meant her father, brothers, Mr Trefusis and his rough but
kindly helpers. The viscount, for she knew it must be him,
was nothing like them. Frock-coat of cashmere, well-cut
trousers and a very expensive waistcoat; he looked like a
god.

Then the sheep were all gone and the coachman had
whipped up the horses. Emily stared after the carriage, the
world suddenly flat and dull. Nothing would ever be quite
the same for her again. Wherever she looked she would see
his face. She would dream of him at night and think about
him during the day. If she wasn't careful he would come
between her and the goal she had set herself.

She forced herself to be sensible, continuing her journey
with slower steps. He was an earl's son. She belonged in a
fisherman's cottage and had just washed the eggs which the
farm hens had laid that day, peeled potatoes for fourteen
people and helped to scrub out the dairy. They lived in
different worlds, and he would have forgotten her already.
Their paths had crossed briefly but now it was over. She
had seen the last of Viscount Asterly.

"Mother." Nicholas was very casual, for the countess
was quick to pick up nuances. "Who was that girl?"

The countess, exquisitely dressed and exuding a faint,
subtle perfume, glanced at her son in mild surprise.

"Girl? Which girl, my dear? I didn't see anyone."

"She was standing by my side of the carriage, waiting for
Jevens to get out of the way."

"Alone?"

"Yes, quite alone."

"Then she must have been one of the farmworkers, or
someone from the village. A person of quality would have
had a chaperon with her. Is it important?"

She was judging his face carefully. Nicholas had never

asked about a girl before. He sensed the danger, dismissing the subject at once.

"No, not at all. I just wondered."

Juliet let the matter go, too. Nicholas was looking bored again; there was nothing to worry about. But if she could have read her son's mind, she would have been filled with dire consternation.

The viscount knew what had happened; it was no good trying to delude himself even if he had to hoodwink others. He was young in years and lacking in experience but he recognised the emotion for what it was. The girl had slid into his heart and she was going to stay there until the day he died. He would grow older and wiser; become a man; marry and have children; inherit his father's title when the time came; take his place in society and make his mark on it. None of it would make any difference.

He would never know true contentment nor the deep fulfilment of holding in his arms the woman he loved. Jevens and his damned sheep had turned his comfortable existence upside down, for on such trivial quirks of destiny hung one's life and future happiness.

"Nicholas!"

Juliet's voice was sharp and he came out of his reverie with a start.

"I'm sorry, did you say something?"

"Yes, twice." The countess was acid. "I asked whether you would like me to invite the Sheridan girl to the ball. Really, you might pay some attention to me."

"Forgive me, mother; I was miles away. I was wondering if Father would let me buy the grey we saw yesterday."

It was a lie, but there was no help for it. He didn't particularly want the horse in question but he had had to think of something quickly. He couldn't let his mother know that he was saying goodbye for ever to the girl with the emerald eyes.

Two weeks later Emily met Harry Pentreath. He was
eighteen, fair-haired, brown-eyed, with a snub nose and a
sunburnt skin.

He lived with his father, two brothers and three sisters in
Devil's Bite, a cove not far from Porthaven. They made
their living by smuggling, but things were getting harder all
the time. Earlier, when England was at war with France
and Spain, the authorities had turned a blind eye to the
Free Traders' activities. Many ships had been granted
licences and had become armed privateers to augment the
naval vessels. They had served their country and themselves
at the same time, making a reasonable living with only the
sea to contend with. It was different now. England was at
peace and the revenue cutters and Preventative boats were
on the watch for them. They lived more precariously, but
somehow managed to make ends meet.

Harry had just delivered some brandy to the local doctor
and had come down the cliff to watch the long-awaited
shoal of pilchards come in. A huer on the headland had
kept vigil for several weeks; now his patience was rewarded
and frantically he signalled the fishermen below, waving his
furze bush to guide them to the right spot.

Harry squatted on a rock, hearing the yell which ordered
the seine to be shot. The large vertical nets were cast,
circling round the silver masses which writhed and twisted
and fought to escape capture.

Then he became aware of Emily, also watching the
feverish scene below. Everyone had come to help; men,
women and children. They filled baskets and rushed them
to the fish-cellars where the pilchards were salted and
stored. After a few weeks they would be pressed to extract
the oil. Some would be dried and kept for home
consumption; most went to Italy where fish on Friday was
the rule.

"You live here?" asked Harry after a moment or two,
quite overcome by the sight of Emily. "I'm from Devil's
Bite, further west."

Emily nodded, noticing Harry for the first time. She knew she should have been on the beach helping, for every single hand counted, but she couldn't face the smell of fish for the moment.

"Yes, I live here. My pa's got a boat. Leaks a bit, but I expect he's caught something."

"Shouldn't you be down there?"

"Yes, and I 'spect I'll get a tanning for staying here, unless Pa's too busy to notice I'm missing."

"Hope he is; too busy, I mean."

She turned her head to meet Harry's grin. He wasn't like the viscount, but he was friendly and she could see the innate kindness in him. Very casually she had asked Miss Pezzach what the earl's son was called. Now she could repeat her love's name over and over again, but only when she was alone. Nicholas had a wonderful ring to it. It was like music to her ears.

"Tell me about yourself."

Harry was surprised at his own boldness, for normally he was shy with girls, but this one was different. Her loveliness made him quake inside and stumble a bit over his words.

Emily hadn't intended to say much, but Harry was a good listener. She found herself telling him everything except, of course, her special and closely guarded secret.

"Sewing sounds dull for a girl like you."

She laughed and Harry was lost. Her voice was low and pleasing, her teeth like a string of pearls he'd once brought over from Cherbourg. As for her body, it made him sweat and he knew she had trapped him as surely as if she had used a net.

"It's not dull and it will get better."

She was animated as she spoke of her future. London, and a small discreet place in the most fashionable part of town. A neat brass plate to indicate her presence; perhaps a single window with a very expensive shawl or fichu in it to entice the weak-willed.

He couldn't follow all that she was saying, but it didn't

matter. He could watch her eyes light up, as if a lamp burnt behind them; see her lips smile in anticipation.

"I'm going to call myself Emerald from now on," she said. "Emily Tregellan is too plain for words. I shall be Madame Emerald. You can call me that if you like."

Harry wriggled uncomfortably.

"I'd feel a fool calling anyone Emerald. Can't I call you Em?"

She considered him for a minute or two. He was nice to be with and perhaps he would stop her from thinking about the viscount.

"All right, as long as you realise Em is short for Emerald and not Emily. What's your name?"

He told her, pleading to see her again. She pretended indifference, for Harry wasn't Nicholas and had to be brought to heel from the beginning.

"If you want to. Do you know the Trefusis farm?"

"No, but I can find it."

"It's near the village of Paul. I work there until seven each night, 'cept on Sundays."

"I'll get there whenever I can. Sometimes, in my business, I have to go away."

She gave him a wink.

"Free Trader, are you? Well, I'm not fussy."

"I'll try and bring you some silk next time I see you."

"I'd like that." Emily's mind was already busily at work planning the cut of the gown she would make from it. "Yellow, if you can; it's my favourite colour, 'cos it's like the sun."

"I'll do me best."

"I'd better go. My luck won't hold for ever."

She blew Harry a kiss and ran lightly down towards the shoreline, her skirts and hair flying. He wanted to call her back and tell her that he loved but his confession would have to wait until next time. He, too, had to get back, or answer to his own father for his dalliance.

Emily was fortunate. No one had missed her and she

slipped into the fish-cellar, swiftly layering the pilchards as if she'd been there all the time. But it wasn't Harry who held her thoughts as her hands reached for more salt. It was Nicholas, who was so handsome that just the memory of his face made her want to cry.

"Emerald," she said to herself, dismissing Emily for good. "You're a fool. Stop mooning over something you can't have and think of a way of making some more money. The sooner you get to London, my girl, the better."

The Trefusis harvest supper was the great autumn event. Everyone who helped on the farm was invited, even those like Emerald who only gave a few hours of their time each day.

Emerald loved the farm kitchen. Mrs Trefusis might have been proud of her hale, or parlour, but it was a stiff, dead room. Its chairs weren't sat on, its table, scrubbed every morning, never had anything put on its pristine surface. The buffette in the corner had painted china behind its glass doors, but even that couldn't bring the place to life.

It was the kitchen, with its huge, cavern-like fireplace, the long tables, the benches, the pots and pans, the dresser filled with pewter and oval dishes and the grandfather clock which wheezed as it struck the hours, which gave Emerald comfort.

Cooking was done much in the same way as Jess did it, but the food produced was quite different. Fresh warm bread, pasties, cakes, scones and roasted meat sprang into view when the ashes were brushed away and the 'baker', or iron bowl, was lifted off. Tender boiled joints and succulent puddings emerged from the pot hanging over the fire which leapt up from its flat stone. Newly churned butter, thick cream and jam were plentiful. There was always beer for the ten men who lived in and tea for the farmer's wife and the other women, like Molly who worked in the dairy.

Morris had been invited too. Not because he worked in the fields or tended the sheep, but because the farmer felt

sorry for him. Whenever Tregellan had fish to sell, Jack
Trefusis bought it from him, pretending he hadn't already
stocked up well for the winter.

Tregellan hadn't wanted to come, but he was afraid of
offending the farmer. Sometimes he suspected that Jack
didn't really need the baskets of pilchards he offered, but he
dismissed the thought quickly. That would have been
charity, and Morris couldn't live with pity.

Emerald looked at her father, the only man with a sullen
expression and nothing to say for himself. Everyone else
was having the time of their lives, chorusing praise as May
Trefusis served the first course.

This year there was beef and mutton, served from crocks
which took two men to hold them. Floury potatoes
accompanied the generous slices of meat and, when the
plates were empty, there came plum puddings, apple
dumplings, fruit tarts and bowls of yellow clotted cream.

The cidar was potent and so was the beer, the women
sipping tea and pretending to scold the men for their
raucous laughter and loose tongues. They didn't really
mind, for 'Guldize', or harvest feast, only came round once
a year.

When it got too hot and noisy, Emerald slipped outside.
It was a pity Harry couldn't have been there to share the
good provender and the friendship openly expressed as
mugs passed from one man to the next. It was even sadder
that the viscount wasn't with her, but he wouldn't have
known what to make of Jack's rowdy companions. He
belonged at the glittering parties which the girls of
Porthaven had described so eloquently.

She didn't hear the step behind her and the first she knew
of the attack was a hand over her mouth, smothering her
cry. Then an arm, round her waist this time, lifting her off
her feet and dragging her into an empty cowshed.

She found herself flung down on the straw, turning to
face her assailant.

"Noah Penrose!" Emerald was furious with the

farmhand for his impudence. "How dare you touch me, you oaf? Help me up this instant or I'll tell master about you."

Penrose leered at her. He was drunk, not even listening to her, and certainly not heeding her threats.

"Pretty Emily." He sniggered. "Want to lie with Noah, do you?"

"No, I don't," she snapped. "Let me past or it'll be the worse for you."

Then all at once it ceased to be a matter of indignation and became a situation of blind panic and fear. The man was strong, holding her still with one hand while he ripped the front of her dress open with the other. She cried out, realising how dangerous he was, feeling suffocated as he pushed her down and lay on top of her.

She fought like a demon, but she was no match for Penrose. She was screaming and struggling as he violated her. First, she was stripped and her breasts roughly fondled. Then his spittle fell on her shrinking flesh as he drooled over her, stroking her white thighs as he forced them apart. Lastly, she felt him thrust into her body, soiling and degrading her as he grunted in satisfaction.

After that she couldn't scream any more. Her throat was parched with her efforts to attract attention, her eyes dazed with terror. All the water in Mounts Bay wouldn't wash her clean after this.

Noah pulled her up, slapping her bottom.

"Nice little bit," he said coarsely. "Think I'll have another helping while I've got the chance."

As she backed away, the viscount seemed to stand before her, cool eyes filled with disdain as he dismissed her as a trollop.

"It wasn't my fault." She wasn't talking to Penrose, but to a boy who wasn't even there. "Please, please believe me! It wasn't my fault."

The next second her father appeared, others peering over his shoulder. His face was thunderous as Penrose staggered across the floor and fled through the open doorway.

Emerald didn't move. She was naked, defenceless and
wholly defeated. She was unaware of the voices which
condemned her; she didn't notice the greedy looks which
swallowed her up.

She was vaguely aware that her father had picked up a
stick, hardly feeling the first blow. Pain was nothing
compared with what had just happened. She didn't care
that more had crowded in to watch her humiliation. She
didn't even see them.

There were red, angry streaks across her back and
buttocks but they didn't count. Her soul and spirit were
crushed, for she was no longer whole.

Her daydreams were over, too. She wouldn't be able to
pretend any more that she and Nicholas were being
married in a big church and that she was wearing the most
perfect dress which she and Oonagh could make. There
were to have been flowers and music and laughter and then
his kiss. Now it was finished. She wasn't a virgin any more
and badgers didn't dream of marrying men like Asterly.

"Get out, girl." Tregellan pulled off his jersey and flung
it at her. "Put that on and then get yourself home, for I
haven't finished with you yet. You're not my daughter any
more and you'll not sleep under my roof for much longer.
May you roast in hell for the shame you've brought on me
this night."

There was a rumble of agreement from those assembled.
Even MrsTrefusis was appalled. Who'd have thought it of a
nice girl like Emily Tregellan? All had judged her and
found her guilty.

Like one in a trance Emerald stumbled along the path
and across the fields, her father behind her. It seemed so
short a time since she had arrived at the farmhouse for the
feast. She had been happy then, wearing a ribbon in her
hair which Miss Pezzach had given her. Now she wished
she were dead.

At fifteen years and one month, Emerald Tregellan,
known to her family as plain Emily, had finished with life.

There was no future for her now; after Noah Penrose, there was nothing left.

Emerald didn't start crying until her father passed final sentence on her. He had told the tale of her disgrace, leaving no detail out. Ancilla gave a shriek, clutching the infant she held as if to spare it from contamination. The boys shuffled uncomfortably; Daisy and Hilda said nothing. Jess coughed into a piece of rag already stained with bright blood.

"The Feverells over at Whitewater want a scullerymaid," said Morris gratingly. He had no idea how he was going to hold up his head in Porthaven again. The curse which had been laid on him at birth was still working against him. "They asked for one of my girls. I was going to send Daisy, seeing she's nine now, but this alters things. You'll go instead."

"No!" Emerald was stricken, her pallor like one dead. Going to Whitewater would mean leaving Oonagh. Her training wasn't finished; she still had things to learn. "Not that, Pa. Anything else, but not that! I can't leave Miss Pezzach. She's teaching me how to sew."

"If she ain't learned you in five years there's not much hope for you."

Morris didn't understand and Emerald couldn't explain things to him. Dressmaking to him was just ordinary woman's work. It didn't conjure up for him the magic of designing gowns for the cream of London society.

"But it wasn't my fault." Emerald was desperate. "I didn't do nothing." She repeated her claim, but she could see that no one believed her. "He did it to me, Pa, I swear. Let me stay; please let me stay."

"You'll leave here in a week." Tregellan ignored her pleading. "You've got to have two black dresses, two aprons and four caps. I'll find a shilling or two from somewhere so you and your precious Miss Pezzach can make 'em up. After that, you'll get nothing more from me.

You'll live on your wages and you'll never come to this cottage again."

"Ma!"

Emerald turned to her mother, hoping against hope that for once Ancilla would support her, but old habits died hard. Ancilla simply lowered her eyes and went on suckling the baby.

"Pa!"

"Shut your mouth." Morris had had enough. "I don't want you sleeping with your sisters neither. Get yourself below to the fish-cellar. You'll stay there till it's time for you to go."

Two hours later Jess crept downstairs, expecting to find Emerald sobbing and distraught.

"Are you all right, Em?"

Emerald gave her sister a cold, reflective look. It seemed to Jess as if she were asking the question of a stranger.

"All right?" Emerald was full of bitter sarcasm. "What do you think? I've been raped by a pig of a man who'll not be called to account for what he's done. Pa whipped me in front of all them up at the farm, and me without a stitch on. Now I'm to go away, so I can't do what I'd set my heart on. You call that all right?"

Jess went on coughing and there were fresh stains on the piece of cloth held against her mouth.

"I'll tell you something, though, Jess." Emerald's voice was as hard as tempered steel. "Next time a man wants me, he's going to have to pay me."

"Em! Don't say such awful things."

"Why not? I've been punished cruelly for something I had no part in. If trying to stay decent gets you where it's got me, I'll try another way. I'll take other men and I'll milk 'em dry."

Jess buried her face in her hands and after a second Emerald said softly:

"Don't take on so. Nothing you can do about it anyway and it seems to me as though you need to look after yourself. You ought to see Dr Lessiter about that cough."

"Ain't got no money for doctors."

"I'll send you some one day."

"No!"

Emerald's smile made her sister draw back.

"Dirty money, eh Jess? Best go now; you don't want Pa finding you here with me."

When she was alone, Emerald leaned against the wall, the smell of fish sickening her. In spite of her conviction that she wouldn't be free to think of the viscount again, she saw his face as clearly as if he were there beside the barrels of pilchards.

"I'm leaving here," she said aloud, closing her eyes in an effort to banish him. "We shan't meet no more, accidental like, for you won't go riding over to Whitewater, will you? Oh, go away and let me be. Sweet Jesus, Nicholas, go away!"

Oonagh listened to Emerald's story in silence, her heart sinking. Her pupil didn't look like a young lady any more; she was a hurt and vulnerable child again.

"My dear, I'm so terribly sorry."

"Well, it's done." Emerald tried to hide her grief, but the warmth and sympathy in which Miss Pezzach was wrapping her was too much for her and tears began to trickle down her cheeks. "I won't be able to come here again and I've so much more to learn. I'll never be a famous dressmaker now."

"Yes, you will, my handsome." Oonagh put aside her own sorrow. Life without Emily was going to be quite dreadful, but it was the girl who mattered now. "Will you get any free time in the situation you're going to?"

"One afternoon a month. Pa said so when he gave me three shillings for my clothes."

"Then you shall come here on that afternoon and we'll go on with our work. It will take longer, but you're so clever and so far advanced that we'll do it right enough."

The green eyes were suddenly filled with hope.

"You mean it, Miss Oonagh? You'll go on helping me, even if I can't pay you back?"

"I don't want you to pay me back, love. I want you to succeed and you will. You won't give up at the first setback. I know you better than you know yourself. You'll get to London in the end."

"Oh, Miss Oonagh!"

Miss Pezzach held Emerald in her arms, crooning and rocking her to and fro as the dam of anguish and despair burst its banks.

When Emerald finally looked up she said in a small voice:

"You don't think I wanted Noah Penrose to ..to ...?"

"Of course I don't. Good gracious, child, do you think I'm a fool? I told you; I know you. You wouldn't do such a thing and I could throttle that brute for what he did. Now, what about the things you have to take with you? Two black frocks was it?"

"And two aprons and some caps. Three shillings won't pay for them but I've got some money in my 'Savings Bag'; I'll use that."

"Indeed you won't. You'll leave that where it is and put the three shillings in there, too. I've enough black serge in the house to make two dozen dresses, besides calico for aprons and linen for caps. Go and wash your face, dear, and then put the kettle on. After that we'll get to work on your clothes. And promise me one thing."

"Yes?"

"Keep your pride and spirit at all costs. In spite of what's taken place, don't give in. You were born to fight; don't disappoint me."

"I won't." At the door Emerald paused. "Miss Oonagh."

"What, my dear?"

"I wish you were my mother."

Miss Pezzach's throat seemed to close and her eyes were

filling rapidly.

"So do I, Emily," she managed at last, "so do I. No woman could have a better daughter than you."

"And I'll fight, like you said." Emerald's lips thinned. "I'll fight very hard. After all, what else is there left for a fallen girl like me to do?"

On the day before she was to leave for Whitewater Emerald met Harry Pentreath. They had managed to see each other once or twice since their first encounter and Harry was totally infatuated with her.

He had been away for a day or two but upon arriving at the farm he was given short shrift. Noah Penrose had been sent packing, but the Tregellan girl was an outcast, too. It was Molly who had come rushing out of the dairy to tell him all about the night of the harvest supper and she who suggested that he should walk over to Paul.

"I want to know who done this." Harry was very grim. "The girl up at the farm said a man had ...had ...well ... but she wouldn't tell me his name. Who was it?"

"Can't tell you, Harry."

"Why not?"

"'Cos you'd do something daft like going after him and that 'ud get you into trouble."

"I don't care about trouble." His hand was tight on her wrist. "Tell me his name."

"No, I've told you I won't. Let it be. And what about you? Do you like everyone else think I'm a strumpet? Everyone 'cept Miss Oonagh, that is."

"Now you're the one talking daft." He was burning with anger at what had been done, chafing because she wouldn't let him avenge her. "You wouldn't have let him near you if you'd had half a chance."

"No, but there weren't no chance."

There was a moment's silence. Then Harry said gently:

"I'm sorry, Em. It must have been ..."

"Yes it was, but I don't want to think about it. I'm going

to the Feverells at Whitewater tomorrow. I'm to be a kitchenmaid. It's funny, isn't it? Me and my grand ideas of being a dressmaker in the West End of London. All I'm going to do is to peel potatoes and scrub floors, just like at home.''

He didn't know what to say, or how to comfort her, but he squeezed her hand and hoped she knew how he felt.

''I know where Whitewater is. I'll come and see you.''

''Shan't be allowed callers, I don't expect.''

''I'll get word to you somehow and you can slip out when it's dark. I can't not see you again, Em, you know that.''

She saw the love in him, because she, too, knew what it was like to love. She wished with all her heart that she could return his feelings, for it would have made everything so simple. They could have got married in time, settled down somewhere along the coast and raised a family. Harry could do a bit of free trading and she could sew for the local women who didn't know how to use a needle.

But she wouldn't cheat him. Whoever else had to pay for Penrose's infamy, it wasn't going to be Harry. Young as she was, Emerald knew that Nicholas Roman was the only man to whom she could ever give her heart.

''All right; I'd like that.''

''I have to go away now and then. Sometimes to Guernsey, sometimes further. You won't think I've deserted you, will you? And I'll bring you back some stuff, like I did before. Even a bottle of perfume, maybe.''

''Never had any perfume. Does it smell sweet?''

''Don't know. Suppose it does, for all them grand women seem to want it.''

Emerald nodded. All the grand and fashionable women who moved in Viscount Asterly's circle, so far away from her.

''Thanks. It 'ud be nice to have some. I'd better go home now.'' She laughed and the sound sent a shudder through him. ''Home! That's a joke, ain't it? Not my home any more and never will be again.''

"Can I kiss you goodbye. I don't mean like ...that is, I wouldn't ..."

His face was brick-red, trying so hard not to injure her further. She gave a smile, quite different in quality to her laugh, as she said gently:

"'Course you can, you great lump."

Their lips met briefly. There was heaven in it for Harry, but Emerald felt nothing. It would take more than a shy salute from Harry Pentreath to start her living again.

He watched her go, returning her wave, sick at heart as he turned in the direction of the cove at Devil's Bite.

"Oh, Em," he said under his breath, feeling a sense of complete helplessness. "What have they done to you, my handsome? Whatever have they done to you?"

THREE

Emerald had expected to hate the Feverells and everything about Rowett Lodge, the family's house at Whitewater.

But she was young and resilient and after a week or two some of her burning resentment had faded. Then interest in what was going on about her quickened again. She missed Oonagh and the dressmaking, but found there were certain compensations in her new job.

The house was the largest Emerald had ever seen. Drawing-room, dining-room, library and parlour below; six bedrooms above, with attics for the servants to sleep in. The kitchen was vast, with rows and rows of copper pans hanging round the walls or perched on shelves. There were bowls for mixing, basins, shakers for sugar and salt, a coffee mill, clockwork spit and much else to aid the preparation of the hearty meals the Feverells enjoyed.

There was no butler, but Mrs Cheadle was an efficient housekeeper, keys rattling at her waist, her sharp eyes everywhere. There was also a cook and two other girls to sweep, dust, polish, scour, empty the chamber-pots each morning and make the beds. The mistress had her own lady's maid, Pudsey, and Betty Jacob, a plump, friendly wench, was nursemaid to the child of the house. Outside, there was Fister, the coachman, Pettifer, the groom and a stableboy.

Jehu Feverell was a self-made man. Although smuggling was reaching the end of its days, due to the vigilance of the excise men, Jehu had started making his money that way

when he was fourteen years old. By his middle years he had
become a successful exporter of pilchards, a trader in seed
and corn, owning mills and lime-kilns, as well as fishing-
smacks which he leased to fishermen he felt he could trust
to look after them.

He was a bluff, hearty man who had married above him,
but Jennet Feverell knew which side her bread was buttered
and lacked for nothing. They had three daughters, Mary,
Meraud and Melanie, well brought up and even polite to
the staff. Roger, the elder son, helped in his father's various
businesses; seldom at home. Nahum was three years old and
spoilt by everyone.

At first, the servants weren't too sure about Emerald,
refusing to call her by such an outlandish name. She was
Em to the maids and Tregellan to the housekeeper and
family. Her fellow workers found her sour of tongue, for she
was far from healed yet, and she might have become
heartily disliked had she not stopped one day to watch
Millie Clopton struggling with a torn sheet.

"Whatever are you doing, Mill?" she asked in
astonishment, putting her polishing cloth down to take a
closer look. "Using a hammer and nails on it, are you?"

Millie was near to tears, for she hated repairing the
household linen and had no aptitude for the task.

"No I'm not," she returned crossly. "I'm turnin' a sheet
edges to middle. See, it's worn in the centre, so I've had to
unpick the hem and ..."

"Well that's not the way."

"Suppose you could do it better, Miss High and
Mighty."

"Certainly couldn't do it worse, could I? Here, leave it
alone. Let me wash my hands and I'll show you how it's
done."

The two maids and Betty Jacob, who had come down for
a cup of tea, gathered round awestruck as Emerald pulled
out Millie's cobbled stitches and began to work. Even cook
stopped making a damson tart to come and watch.

No one spoke, every eye fixed on the small white hands which moved so deftly and accurately along the seam, for they had never seen anything like it before.

"Not best quality sheeting," observed Emerald as she finished and snipped off the thread. "About five shillings and threepence a yard, I'd say."

"Where did you learn to sew like that?" Cook, a round, pleasant woman called Duckworth, was studying the stitches, hardly able to see them. "Didn't pick that up by yourself, I'll be bound."

Emerald winked at her.

"No, I had a bit of help. Anything more wants mending?"

Millie, who was just beginning to recover, pointed to a large wicker basket full of pillow cases, towels, dressing-table covers, tablecloths and napkins and some dozen or so pantry aprons.

"All them, and I'll never get through 'em in time. Mrs Cheadle says I'm as slow as a funeral and if I don't buck my ideas up I'll have to go."

Emerald didn't mince her words.

"She's right. A tortoise could move faster 'un you. Go and peel those spuds for me while I deal with this lot. Floss, can you finish rubbing up them brass kettles for me?"

Floss could, for she was Millie's friend and didn't want to see her lose her position. The others felt the same, even Mrs Duckworth giving a hand when she had got her pies and cakes ready for the Dutch oven. It seemed no time at all before all the mending was done, every last piece finished to a standard never before seen at Rowett Lodge.

After that Emerald did all the mending, the rest of the servants sharing most of her work, even Betty Jacob pitching in when her charge was asleep. It made Emerald very popular, particularly when she took to catching up the hem of a dress for one, stitching a new shift for another, making a petticoat for Betty and a nightgown for cook.

She was almost happy again, glad to feel material

between her hands, a needle between thumb and finger. She was deferred to, given titbits by cook, looked up to even by Pudsey, for whom she had trimmed a bonnet.

When she heard the others talking about the Earl of Radfield and his family, Emerald pricked up her ears. She hadn't been able to stop thinking about Nicholas after all and, that being so, she was hungry for news of him.

The staff always had plenty to say about the earl and countess, for they were the most important people for many miles around and all agreed there was no better-looking young man in England than Viscount Asterly. Very occasionally Emerald would ask a casual question about him, pretending the answer meant nothing to her. It hurt when they spoke of the high-born fillies who admired him; gladdened her heart when she learned he wasn't interested in the female of the species.

Six months later Mrs Feverell discovered who it was who had been doing the mending so expertly.

She was a small woman with pale brown hair and hazel eyes. Her clothes were expensive, but, to Emerald's critical eye, not smart. As she stood in front of her mistress waiting for her to speak, she was mentally redressing Jehu's wife in amber-coloured mousseline-de-laine with a brown velvet trim.

"It's quite extraordinary," said Jennet finally. "I've never seen stitches as tiny as this before. How do you see them?"

"Clearly enough, madam. Not difficult when you know how."

"But so few people know how."

Mrs Feverell put the nightcap aside and gave Emerald a thoughtful look. She didn't often go down to the kitchen and had only seen the new maid once or twice. She couldn't imagine how she had failed to see the girl's loveliness. Black serge, white apron and cap, under which raven locks could just be seen, only seemed to enhance Tregellan's appearance. Her gaze dropped to the slender white hands, beginning to shew signs of Emerald's labours with the saucepans and pots, for the latter still helped out now and then with such chores.

"I've had it in mind for some time now to give the girls a maid to themselves," she said musingly. "Pudsey is getting on a bit and she can't really cope with more than me. Besides, my daughters are growing up. Mary's nearly nineteen, Meraud's seventeen and Melanie will be fifteen soon. If you became their maid, you could sew for them, couldn't you? Not just mending, I mean. You could make some of the simpler garments as well."

Emerald felt excitement lick through her.

"I could make more than simple things, ma'm. I made the dress I'm wearing."

Mrs Feverall paused.

"Well, yes, but I think Mrs Chessington will have to go on doing the girls' gowns. They're not quite the same thing as a maid's dress. Would you like the post?"

Emerald wanted it most passionately, but her ambition was flourishing again. Nicholas Roman was beyond her grasp, but London wasn't and she needed money. She didn't think it would be too long before her mistress realised that the girls' ballgowns were child's play to their new maid. It would be more experience to add to her monthly afternoon with Miss Oonagh.

"Very much, ma'm, but I would need a larger wage."

"Of course." Jennet was somewhat taken aback. There had been a very positive note in Tregellan's voice. "I should expect that, but you're young. You can't expect anything like I pay Pudsey."

"Miss Pudsey doesn't sew; I will."

For a second or two Mrs Feverell was almost irritated; then she laughed.

"You're like my husband; he always got what he wanted. I don't think Jehu ever took no for an answer in his life. All right, fourteen pounds a year to begin with, then we'll see. Does that satisfy you?"

"For the moment, ma'm. When shall I start?"

"Today, for I can see there'll be no holding you. I'll tell the girls at teatime and then you can help them dress for dinner."

Emerald went down to the kitchen with flushed cheeks. She had finished with potatoes and copper pans and turning sheets sides to middle. She would have the chance to study the materials the girls' dresses were made of; see her mistress's gowns too, and those of her visitors, if she peered over the banister rail without getting caught. She didn't expect to be unduly impressed by any of them, but they would be worth looking at if only to avoid making mistakes herself.

As for Mrs Chessington's handiwork, that was dismissed very promptly. The dressmaker didn't know her job, or the mistress would look a sight better than she did now. It wouldn't happen overnight, of course, but Emerald could afford to wait and while she waited she could save.

She had promised Miss Pezzach she would keep her pride and her spirit and she had. She was back on the right road again and at the end of it was London.

"Mill," she said as she sat round the table with her companions to sample Mrs Duckworth's saffron cake, "I'm going to have to teach you a bit of plain sewing, for I shan't have time for it after today. I'm going to be a lady's maid. Now what do you think of that?"

A year went by and Emerald hardly noticed it go. She was working very hard but loved every minute of what she was doing. She saw Oonagh regularly and met Harry whenever she could.

Jennet thought her daughters' maid was the most attractive girl she'd ever seen, watching her blossom in her new happiness. Jehu noticed Emerald too, marking the sensual movements of her body and feeling sheer, unadulterated lust whenever he was near her.

When Harry told her that his father was pressing him to

marry Deborah Lovell, daughter of a man with whom he wished to go into partnership, Emerald was strangely unmoved. Her affection for Harry was genuine but she didn't love him. She had to face the fact that if he ever overcame his marked reluctance to wed the girl, he wouldn't be able to get over to Whitewater at nights so that she could slip out and talk to him. There wouldn't be any more pieces of French material or perfume either, but it didn't bother her. What held her mind and heart in thrall was the thought of Nicholas. She had only seen him once, and for such a short time, yet the memory of him remained as fresh and exciting as ever.

Things might have gone on as they were for some time had not Nahum fallen into a large pond in the gardens of Rowett Lodge. Betty Jacob had returned to the house for something, leaving the boy some distance from the water. But when Emerald was returning from the village and crossing the lawn she could hear his screams.

She ran as fast as she could and as she drew closer it was obvious that the child was near to drowning. She threw her reticule and basket aside and plunged into the pond. It was deep and the boy was fighting her, but Emerald was a strong swimmer. By the time help arrived she had got Nahum on dry land and was slapping him on the back to force him to throw up the slime he had swallowed.

"Mr Feverell and I can never thank you enough," said Jennet some hour later. "Nahum is the child of our autumn. We shan't have any more, for I'm past such things and so is my husband."

Emerald, who had observed the glint in Jehu's eye, doubted it very much. He was a lecher if ever she'd seen one.

"He's the apple of our eye," Mrs Feverell went on, still trembling from the fright she had received. "There is no way we can really repay you, Tregellan, but I want you to take this length of material as a small token of our gratitude. As you can see, it is the finest jaconet to be had."

Emerald gave a small curtsy, thanking Mrs Feverell for
the gift. It was yellow, her special colour, and tomorrow
was her half-day. She would take it with her to Oonagh's
and cut it out. She wouldn't bother with a pattern, for she
had her own ideas about how it should look. It was an
opportunity to shew her mistress what high fashion really
meant.

Since Emerald had quite a lot of spare time as ladies'
maid to Jehu's daughters, it took no longer than a week to
complete the dress. The bodice had a sharply-pointed
waist, the skirt full, elaborate and shaped like a bell. The
sleeves billowed to the elbow and then tightened towards
the wrist, à la Donna Maria; a fichu of fine lace completed
the picture.

Emerald put the gown on, pinning her hair up high and
went downstairs to see what Mrs Duckworth, Millie and
the others made of her achievement.

At first no one said a word. They just gaped at the vision
in front of them like deaf mutes. Then at last Millie
whispered:

"Em, wherever did you get that from?"

"I told you. Mrs Feverell gave me the material for fishing
young Master Nahum out of the pond."

"But who made it up?" Cook moved nearer to study the
details of the outfit. "You never did this yourself."

"Yes, I did." Emerald twirled round, delighted by the
sensation she had caused. "Like it, do you?"

At last they recovered their voices, all talking at once.

"Em, it's wonderful."

"Look at them flounces, Floss."

"Em, can you make me one like that?"

"See the size of the sleeves, Mrs D."

"What about this lace, Betty?"

Emerald felt warm inside. She had conquered the kitchen
and was prepared to be generous.

"Yes, I'll make you all one, any kind you like. Just give

me the stuff and I'll get on with it, but you'll have to pay me."

She said much the same thing to Mrs Feverell when the latter, hearing rumours of the fabulous gown, demanded that Emerald should put it on and let her see it.

"It's everything I've heard said of it." Jennet shook her head in disbelief as she examined every seam. "It's the finest work I've ever seen and you are quite ravishing. Did you have a pattern for this?"

"No, ma'm. It's my own design."

"I see." Jennet was meditative. The girl had been right and she had been wrong. Tregellan could do much more than sew a simple shift. "Will you make clothes for me and my daughters? Mrs Chessington is able enough, but this looks as though it has come straight from Paris."

"I'd be glad to." Emerald felt the surge of triumph she had waited for for so long, "but ..."

Jennet chuckled.

"But I'll have to pay you more."

"Yes ma'm, you will."

Mrs Feverell's smile faded.

"You're not an avaricious girl, I can tell that. Why is money so important to you?"

"Because of what I want to do one day."

"May I know what that is, or shouldn't I ask?"

"I want to go to London when I'm older and open a shop. Not an ordinary place, but one where only the aristocracy go to buy their clothes."

"I see. Yes, that will take money and hard work." Her eyes met Emerald's. "I think you'll succeed, but I hope you won't go too soon. I have the prettiest piece of flowered muslin you ever saw and I want the best ballgown in the county."

"You shall have it, ma'm. I'll take the measurements tomorrow, if I may. Then I'll show you some sketches and you can choose the style, but if I don't think it will suit you,

I shall say so.''

Jennet laughed again.

"I don't doubt it for a second, my dear, but I'll put myself in your hands. Just take the measurements and then do what you want. I shan't be disappointed, I know that.''

Emerald put her sunshine gown away, stroking it fondly. It had opened the right door for her, and Mrs Feverell's terms were generous. Yet as she lay staring into the darkness that night it wasn't London which Emerald was thinking about, nor her future shop.

She was wondering if the viscount would have liked the dress, could he have seen it, and whether he would have said she was ravishing as Jennet had done.

She would never know and she forced him out of her mind with a gentle rebuke, her body yearning for his.

"Go away, Nicholas, my love; go away. I can't have you, so leave me be. For pity's sake, leave me alone.''

Whilst Emerald went on longing for Nicholas Roman, Harry Pentreath's love for her deepened.

He had resisted vehemently the idea of marrying Deborah Lovell, thus incurring the wrath of his own father as well as that of Edgar Lovell, who regarded Harry's attitude as a slight on his daughter.

Deborah Lovell was a plump girl, rosy-cheeked, fair-haired with queer round eyes and lips fixed in an almost permanent pout. She, too, had been mightily incensed by Harry's obstinacy. Unlike her father and Victor Pentreath, however, she was not prepared to rely merely on exhortations and pleadings.

"I'm going to have him, Keziah," she said to her sister. "I'll not let him make a fool of me. Everyone in the village is laughing at me because I can't even hook a fish like Harry and I won't have it.''

Keziah, a quiet girl two years older than Deborah, was wary. She didn't like her sister very much, knowing how sly and cunning she could be. Deb could twist their father round her little finger and always manzged to place the blame on others if anything went wrong.

"What can you do?" asked Keziah, watching the pout grow more pronounced. "It's clear he's not for marrying you and you don't love him."

Deborah turned her head and Keziah felt cold.

"You're wrong, I do love him. Don't know why, for there's plenty better looking and with more to offer who'd be glad to have me. Don't seem to matter, 'cos I want Harry."

Keziah doubted if Deborah had really loved anyone in her life except herself, yet there was something different about her and it was frightening. Deb was capable of doing almost anything to get her own way.

Deborah's first move was to visit Porthaven, where she enquired where the Tregellans lived. Keziah went with her reluctantly, not sure what she was in for, but she soon found out.

They met Jess Tregellan coming up from the beach towards the cottage. She was like a wraith, with no flesh on her and near to death. It didn't occur to her that there was anything wrong in telling the bouncy, smartly dressed girl that Em was working for the Feverells at Whitewater. She had no idea why the question had been asked and she didn't really care.

Keziah made a token protest as their carriage bowled along the road to Whitewater. She was certain her sister was bent on making trouble for someone, but she wasn't sure who was to be the victim.

"Why are we going to Whitewater, Deb?" she asked for the fourth time. "I don't see ..."

"No, you don't, blind-eyes, but I'll tell you. I've heard the gossip about Harry and Emily Tregellan, even if your ears have been stuffed up. I want to see what she looks like; then I'll decide what's to be done."

"You can't do anything if Harry loves her."

Deborah's smile was hateful.

"Watch me. No one's ever taken anything away from me that I want, and no one's going to now."

Keziah grew more uneasy than ever. Deb was right. What Deborah wanted, Deborah got, and she held on to it.

They didn't have to go up to Rowett Lodge, for when they reached the village Deborah ordered the coachman to stop. Then she alighted daintily and smiled at a respectable-looking woman passing by, seeking confirmation.

"Why, yes, miss. Emily Tregellan does work at the big house. Matter of a fact she's in the village at this very moment. In that shop over there what sells cottons and things."

Deborah got back into the carriage and waited, her sister fidgeting by her side. When Emerald emerged from the shop, studying her list, Keziah could feel the hatred emanating from Deb as if she were sitting next to a red-hot fire.

On the way home Deborah made her plans.

"I shall tell Harry that the girl's left Rowett Lodge. I'll say she's moved on to another post."

"But that's a lie."

"No one will know that, because you'll back me up. You'll confirm we were told she'd gone."

"Deb! I can't."

The eyes, as round and glassy as marbles, met Keziah's and the latter felt another shiver run through her.

"You'll do it, Kez, unless you want there to be an accident."

"Accident? I don't know what you mean."

"Fluff, that stupid dog of yours: pity if it got itself killed. You'd miss him, wouldn't you?"

Keziah was beaten before she started and when Deborah gave Harry the news, Keziah nodded unhappily.

"It's true, Harry, she's moved on."

But Harry Pentreath wasn't a fool and he had the measure of Deborah Lovell. He was thankful that he had refused to take her for a wife. She was spiteful and dangerous and if he'd married her he would never have had a minute's peace, wondering what she was up to. It wouldn't have taken Deb long to find out about his friendship with Em; people had seen them together and tongues wagged.

He was certain that Em would have got word to him had she been planning to leave Whitewater and he wasn't surprised to find, when he went to that village himself, that Em was still working for the Feverells. He got hold of the stableboy, who always obliged by getting a note to Em in exchange for a copper.

He would see Em tomorrow night, but his happiness would be marred. He was scared for her, because he'd read in Deborah's unwavering gaze a message which froze him to the marrow. He didn't understand why Deb was so beset with the idea of becoming his wife, for he had no conceit about himself, but of one thing he was now convinced.

If Deb wanted him she would fight for him and if Em got in the way almost anything could happen to her. The only sure way he could protect Em was to stop seeing her and marry Deb, but he wasn't ready to face that yet. That was a momentous decision for another day and slowly he went back to Devil's Bite, the slouch of his shoulders measuring his despair.

"Nicholas, have you thought any more of the matter we were discussing the other day? I mean about the Marquis of Bracknell's daughter."

Viscount Asterly had just come in from a morning ride, very splendid in a riding-coat, the front skirts of which sloped away abruptly from above the waist, forming broad tails behind, with a vent, hip buttons and pleats. His trousers fitted tightly to his long, sinewy legs; his cravat was perfectly tied.

"Can't say I have, my lord." He turned to look at the Earl of Radfield, a tall, thin man with a clever face and keen eyes. "Damn it, I'm not yet twenty."

"I wasn't suggesting you should do more than consider the proposal at this stage. The girl's only fifteen."

"Dear God! Are you trying to make a cradle-snatcher of me?"

The earl was patient, for marriage between his heir and the marquis's daughter, Frances, was important to him.

"You know I'm not; don't be tiresome. I'm asking you to agree to the marriage when the time is propitious."

"I might turn the idea over in my mind." The viscount gave his father a wink. "Meanwhile, I'm going to sow a few wild oats as you did when you were my age."

"I've no objection to that." The earl shrugged. "You wouldn't be normal if you didn't want to follow in my steps in that regard, but be careful how you choose the women you sleep with."

"I always am." Asterly looked amused. "I've no wish to get the pox."

"I'm not talking about loose women, but our own kind. Pick those who know the rules of the game. I don't want you backed into a corner by some over-zealous mother."

"I won't be." Nicholas's voice had grown very soft. "I'll marry with great care."

When he had left the room, the earl frowned. There had been something in the way his son had spoken which bothered him. It sounded as though the marquis's fifteen-year-old daughter was very far from Asterly's thoughts. He took counsel with his wife, who was shrewd, wise and always fully conversant with any gossip which was going about.

"My dear, you worry too much," said Juliet calmly. "How can you expect the boy to take seriously a matrimonial venture so far into the future? Good heavens, Selwyn, remember what you were like at nineteen. You were the most notorious rake in London. I know, because I was keeping an eye on you."

Radfield was diverted for a moment.

"Were you? Why?"

"Because I intended to marry you, of course. I let you have your fling and then I snared you."

The earl laughed and raised her hand to his lips.

"Hussy, and I thought I was making the running."

"How foolish men are."

Radfield's smile faded.

"Yes, they are, and that's what bothers me. Nicholas spoke just now as if there was a woman somewhere."

"There are probably several, if I know my son."

The earl shook his head.

"No, I don't mean that. He spoke quietly and as if he were in love."

"If there was anyone of particular importance I would know about it," said Juliet with a derisive smile. Really, Selwyn was being positively obsessional about Bracknell's daughter. "I can tell you the names of each woman he's slept with and every girl he's looked at twice. Shall I list them for you?"

The earl relaxed. If there had been someone special, Juliet would have been in possession of every last detail concerning the female involved.

"No, but keep your ear to the ground and your eyes open."

"I always do," returned the countess suavely, reaching up to kiss her husband. "How do you think I managed to catch you?"

That afternoon Nicholas Roman went riding again, accompanied by his father's groom. It wasn't the first time he'd taken the road to Porthaven and it wouldn't be the last, but hitherto he'd met with no success.

It seemed an eternity since he'd seen the dark-haired girl with the green eyes, yet in another way only yesterday. He had never put her completely out of his mind, the brief meeting and the long separation adding fuel to his longing. It made her mysterious and unattainable and therefore impossible for forget.

Oxford had filled part of the intervening time, London the rest. Now he was home for a while but before he went on with his life in the capital he had to see her once more.

He hoped she would have changed. The lot of fisherfolk was a hard one. She had probably lost her looks in the grinding poverty which beset so many of the small villages round the coast. He knew where she had been making for that day long ago. When his mother and father weren't listening, he'd asked the coachman which way he thought she was going. The man had seen her before, in Porthaven, so there could be no mistake. If she had lost her beauty, weary and dejected with toil, perhaps he would be able to cut loose the strings which tied him to her.

She might have married and had children. The thought of that sent such a sharp stab of rejection through him that he almost exclaimed aloud. She couldn't marry anyone else; she was his.

Murdock McFee, the earl's groom, had taught the viscount how to ride, shoot and fish. There was great affection between the two men, and McFee was discretion itself, if blunt of tongue.

He listened to Asterly's tale, rubbing his chin.

"I'll go and ask a few questions," he said. "Don't suppose there's all that number of wenches as fair as this one is, according to you."

"According to anyone." Nicholas laughed. "I'd have forgotten her by now if she'd been ordinary."

When Murdock came back with the news that Emily Tregellan fitted the description, and that she was working at Rowett Lodge in Whitewater, the viscount was in a fever to get there.

"Can't march up to the front door and ask to see her, can you?" Murdoch was very down to earth. "She's a servant, m'lord. Think of the scandal."

"I have been thinking of it; that's why I've never

enquired about her in Porthaven myself. It's why I brought you with me today."

"Is it indeed?"

"Yes. I've wanted to ask for your help many times before but it wasn't until this morning that I screwed up the courage to do so. I thought you'd think me a fool. And perhaps I won't have to knock at her door. She might be out walking, or in the garden. I won't speak to her, I promise. I just want to see her and, God willing, lay a ghost."

McFee studied the look on Asterly's face and was surprised. Proper young rascal was Master Nicholas, from all he'd heard about the viscount's activities in London. Didn't make sense that he wanted to find a fisherman's brat he'd only seen once before. Still, the hurt was real enough and Murdoch nodded.

"All right, we'll go to Whitewater, but watch your step. If the earl got to hear about this he'd have plenty to say."

"Not as much as my mother would. Come on, Murdoch. I've waited three years; I'm not going to wait another minute."

When they reached Rowett Lodge, McFee dismounted.

"I'm going to sit meself down here and have a smoke of me pipe. You go on and see if she's in the grounds or the lane, but if she's not, that's an end of it."

"You sound like a gaolor."

"I am and don't you be forgetting it. Off with you."

Asterly didn't expect for one moment that fortune would smile on him or that Emily, his lost girl, would be in the garden of her employer's house. He was shaken when he drew close to the fence. A group of young women were laughing together as they played ball with a boy, the latter rolling about on the grass in delight.

When Emerald looked up and saw the man on horseback she knew immediately who it was. He was some distance away and he wasn't sixteen any longer, but she needed no one to tell her it was the viscount. She made an apology to

the others, but they were too busy frolicking to hear her.
Then she walked slowly across the lawn until she reached
the fence.

He was even more handsome than she had remembered;
very sophisticated now. There was knowledge in the eyes
which met hers, but the skin was the same light tan, the
bones of cheek and jaw as perfect as before.

Nicholas was transfixed. She hadn't changed into a
work-worn woman, old before her time. She was
breathtaking from the top of her glossy hair to the tips of
her shoes, half-hidden beneath a gown of printed cotton.
She had filled out slightly, but not too much. Time had
rounded her breasts and hips delightfully, but he could
have spanned her tiny waist with his hands.

They went on gazing at each other, quite content to
remain silent. Both knew that there was nothing to say and
no way of remedying their predicament. It was enough that
they were a few feet apart; sufficient that they could drink
their fill of each other.

Emerald felt exactly the same sensation as she had done
on the first occasion she had seen him. It was like making
love again. A sensual, passionate, exciting union, as if they
were naked in bed with hands exploring, lips meeting
avidly. It was the same for Asterly and he felt the chill of
defeat on him. She remained the girl of his fantasies and he
still loved her with the same terrible, destructive force.

He had hoped it had been a boyhood illusion but it was
real and Emerald saw his jaw tighten, knowing exactly
what he was thinking.

When Melanie called to her she knew she had to go. He
knew it too, gripping the reins of his mount a fraction
tighter. Then he turned away and in a minute or two was
gone. Emerald felt as if all the strength had drained out of
her, sucked dry by such fierce emotion.

She had seen him again, as she had prayed so hard she
would, and she knew he had wanted the meeting just as
much. She had read the need in him, for it was like her own,

but there was one thing Viscount Asterly didn't know and her face was ashen as she walked slowly back to Melanie, Mary and Meraud.

He didn't know about Noah Penrose. She was living that night over again as she walked the last few yards. The gross hands on her flesh, the agony, the sickening loss of something which had been precious to her. Making love with Nicholas wouldn't be like that. He would be gentle at first, she knew that. He would whisper in her ear of how he felt about her, soft but demanding fingers rousing her until she was half-mad with desire, and then ...

"Em, what's wrong?"

It was as if someone had slapped her face to bring her round from a swoon and Emerald stared at Melanie in shock.

"Em dear, you're as white as a sheet." Meraud this time, taking Emerald's arm. "Are you ill? Let's go back to the house and get some water."

"I'm ...I'm all right." She managed to get the words out at last, frightened in case the girls had seen anything. "Yes, I did feel a bit giddy, but it's passed off now. I'm as right as rain, truly I am. Now, Master Nahum, where's that ball of yours?"

FOUR

From the time Emerald started to make gowns for Mrs
Feverell and her daughters her work had got better and
better. Practice made perfect and Emerald had plenty of
that. When Jennet's friends begged her to allow her maid to
create outfits for them she had agreed, warning them
laughingly that they'd have to pay generously for her
services,

"Not much more I can teach you, my dear," said
Oonagh one afternoon. "You're better than I ever was.
Keep working, though. You learn something new every
time you pick up a length of material. Never think you
know it all; no one ever does."

Emerald hadn't seen the viscount again and weeks had
gone by, the joy and sadness of their meeting locked up in
her heart. Once or twice the servants mentioned him and,
much to her surprise, so had Harry.

"You know him?" she had asked, trying not to sound too
incredulous, for that might have aroused his suspicions.
"He lives a tidy way from Devil's Bite, doesn't he?"

Harry had winked and laid a finger along the side of his
nose.

"I gets about quite a bit, and it ain't just the doctor at
Porthaven who's glad to see my wares. Why, do you know
him, too?"

" 'Course not. Millie and the others talk about the earl
and his family sometimes, that's all. What's he like?"

"Decent enough cove. Fact, come to think of it, he's very

friendly for an earl's son. Always speaks kindly, if you know what I mean. Handsome, too.''

The conversation had ended there, for Emerald was afraid to pursue it, but it encouraged her to think that precious scraps of information might be culled from Harry now and then, as well as from the staff.

Apart from her wages and the extra money which Mrs Feverell's friends paid her, Emerald had been given permission to turn out a few things for the local shop. Nothing fancy or expensive; just simple shirts, shifts, aprons and caps, but each was made into something special by the skill of her fingers. Jennet knew how much Emerald wanted to save and she admired the girl for her industry and dedication.

Things went on quite smoothly until one day Mrs Feverell went to visit her sister in Surrey, taking the girls and Nahum with her. Jehu stayed at home for, as he told Jennet, he had far too much to do to go gallivanting about the countryside. Roger had been dispatched to visit his godmother, a wealthy eccentric who was worth placating for what she would one day leave him in her will. Even Mrs Cheadle had gone for a day or two to visit a sick friend in Bournemouth.

The house was quiet. Jehu went out early, never returning much before eight at night. The servants took their time about their work, relishing their comparative freedom, stopping to chat and raid the tea caddy. Emerald continued to sew and dream of Nicholas.

One night she glanced at the clock and found it was nearly midnight. She had been so absorbed in what she was doing that she had felt no fatigue or sense of passing time. She hung up the morning gown and started to undress. She was down to her shift when she heard the door open and turned quickly. She had a room of her own now and normally the servants never ventured into it without an invitation.

She stared at Jehu Feverell for a long time, the seconds

ticking by. She had read him for what he was as soon as she'd seen him but had thought herself safe while Mrs Feverell and the girls were in the house. Now they weren't there and Jehu was making the most of his opportunities.

At first she was paralysed, back in the cowshed with Noah Penrose. Then her mind steadied as she saw his smile.

She knew she had to make a decision and her review of the options open to her was swift and to the point. If she refused him he would find an excuse to dismiss her. He wouldn't dare let her remain at Rowett Lodge in case she told Mrs Feverell about his extra-marital activities.

Leaving Whitewater, probably without a reference, would mean going quite a long way away to find another post. Jehu would spread rumours about her locally; she couldn't stay in the district after that. She would no longer be able to get to Oonagh's once a month. More important still, she might have to go so far off that there would never be another chance of catching a glimpse of Nicholas. She had looked for him every time she went into the garden, but she hadn't seen him again. Yet there was always hope, provided she stayed where he knew he could find her.

On the more practical side, she was no longer a virgin. Jehu wouldn't be robbing her of her maidenhead; she'd lost that already. Even if the viscount rode past the house a hundred times a day she could never have him except in her imagination. Lastly, since she couldn't have the man she loved, she might as well increase her earnings and settle for success. As she had once said to Jess, any man who took her now would have to pay.

Feverell crossed the room, eyes roaming over her. He'd wanted her almost from the day she had arrived but there had never been any hope of enjoying her before. There might never be such a chance again, and he cleared his throat.

"I've been watching you, Em. That's what the other servants call you, isn't it?"

"Yes, but my name's Emerald." She was very cool, knowing she had to control the situation from the beginning. "In this room, that's what you'll call me."

Jehu rumbled with laughter. He'd been right about this wench; a real honey-pot and brimming full of spirit. He liked women with a bit of go in them; they were more fun to tame between the sheets.

"All right, Emerald, I've been watching you."

"I know. I've watched you watching me."

"Saucebox. Ought to put you over my knee for your impudence."

"But you won't, not unless I want you to."

"Hoity-toity." He stretched out a hand and touched her shoulder, feeling her skin warm and unbelievably smooth. "You've got a rough tongue, lass."

"I've got an even rougher temper and don't touch me until we've agreed terms."

Jehu stopped smiling, his heavy brows knitting together.

"Terms? What are you talking about? What terms?"

"The terms on which you'll fornicate with me."

"Here, less of that."

"Want it wrapped up, do you?" She was scornful. "Call it what you like; it's still fornication. Listen, master, I don't do anything for nothing. Ask your wife; she knows. I'll pleasure you, if you like, but you'll have to pay and pay well."

"You bloody trull!" He was furious. He had never fouled his own doorstep before, but there were a number of women in his employ, any of whom was ready and willing to give him what he wanted. They considered it an honour to be chosen by him and he regarded it as right and proper that they should. "I've a mind to throw you out neck and crop."

"As you wish."

Very slowly Emerald let the shift slip inch by inch down to her waist and Jehu swallowed hard. It was a long time since he'd seen anything as lovely as his wife's maid and the provocative way in which she had removed the garment

made his loins burn. He didn't move as she finished
undressing, standing before him as bold as brass as she
named her price.

"Well, am I worth it?"

He took a deep breath. She'd beaten him and they both
knew it. He couldn't leave the room without taking her.

"All right, all right." He was fumbling with his jacket
buttons. "Get into bed."

"Money first – on the table over there. Then I'll get into
bed."

Jehu began to laugh again. He liked a worthy adversary
and never held a grudge against those who got the better of
him fair and square. This young madam had certain done
that and he could hardly wait to get his clothes off, hot for
the feel of her body against his.

He put the money down and Emerald nodded.

"Good, and it'll be the same next time."

"Going to be a next time, is there?"

"I expect so, don't you? Mistress isn't due back for two
weeks." Her smile was as wicked as it was enticing. "Well,
come on. You've paid your dues. What are you waiting
for?"

Jehu came back, as Emerald had known he would. She
was everything he had hoped she'd be and he was trying to
work out a way of seeing her at night after his family
returned.

Emerald gave him fair exchange for his guinea, but she
hated every moment he was with her. She steeled herself to
smile and flirt with him, wondering what the viscount
would say if he could see her. She really was a Cyprian
now, by her own choice, and Nicholas would despise her for
it. She fought back tears, gritting her teeth as the door
closed behind Feverell. Then she started to wash herself all
over, rubbing hard as if she were covered with pitch.

It didn't matter what the viscount thought. He had no
part to play in her life. What she was doing with Jehu was
just another means of earning money; money which would

get her where she wanted to go.

It was only after she lay down again, head buried in the pillow, that she was honest with herself.

"Nicholas," she whispered, feeling the heavy hand of Feverell still on her. "I'm sorry, I'm sorry. There isn't any other way for me; try to understand. I can't have you, so nothing else matters. Oh, my dearest dear, I do love you so very much."

"Christ! Are you sure? You could be wrong."

Emerald's gaze was steady and suddenly Jehu Feverell looked years older. His cheeks seemed to have sunk in, his jowels quivered.

"There's no mistake. I'm pregnant."

"God Almighty, you'll have to go?"

"Go where?"

"Anywhere. Just get out of my house."

"Carrying your bastard with me?"

"No one would believe it was mine."

"Your wife would." Emerald was crisp and assured. This was a contest she couldn't afford to lose. "I'd explain one or two of the things you did in bed. She might recognise some of your ways. Might start her wondering, too, whether I was the first. I've heard tell that her brothers didn't want her to marry you; said you were beneath her. They'd listen to me, don't you reckon?"

"You ... you ...!"

The little cow was right. Jennet's two brothers had opposed the match until the very day of the wedding. They were important men and would jump at the chance of ruining him in his business ventures.

"What are you going to do about it, Mr Feverell?"

"Do? How should I know? Do you want the child?"

She looked at him with contempt. He was like a pricked bladder, his self-confidence diminishing as he tried to fight his way out of the trap. He was no longer the master who had to be respected, and his joviality had vanished along with his lust. He was just an ageing man facing disaster; a feeble creature whose seed she carried in her womb.

"Of course I don't want it but I've no choice, have I? Still, I'll tell you this. You're not turning me out to starve."

He was hating her with his eyes, but he knew he couldn't scare her off, as he'd done others in the past. From the moment he'd gone to her room that night he had known she was different.

"No, no, of course not." He pulled himself together. She couldn't stay with him in the library much longer. Jennet or one of the girls might come in and find them together. He had to get rid of her quickly.

"There's an old woman over Trethewey way. She'll help."

"Like she's helped your other doxies? How does she do it?"

He looked savage but his colour was returning to normal as a way out of the dilemma opened up before him. He was a fool not to have thought of it before.

"I don't ask, I just pay."

"How can I get there? It's too far to walk."

"I'll see you get there. Her name's Mother Bonny and I'll send word to her that you're coming. When's your next afternoon off?"

"Monday."

"Then I'll arrange it for that day. Go to the village and wait by the inn at two o'clock. A cart will pick you up and the driver will give you the money."

"You trust him?" She gave a derisory smile. "'Spect you do. Won't be the first time he's done the journey, eh?"

"That's none of your business. Well, do you agree?"

Emerald hesitated. Her instinct to reject the plan was very strong. Just the mention of Mother Bonny frightened her. A local wise woman with the ability to snuff out life: it made goose-pimples come up on her arms. Then she stifled her disquiet. There wasn't an alternative; an infant didn't fit in with her plans. If it had been Nicholas's child, conceived in love, it would have been quite different. She would have done anything to protect his baby.

"Very well," she said, still calm on the surface. "On one condition."

"You aren't in a position to make conditions."

"Neither are you, master."

He backed off from the fight; this girl could destroy him.

"What do you want?"

"To stay here for a while and go on working for Mrs Feverell. I'm not ready to leave yet, but it won't be long."

"Not a word to anyone, mind. Your oath on that."

"Not likely to boast about a thing like this, am I? Yes, I promise."

She left him, going back to her room, trying not to think about Mother Bonny. She picked up a book from the bedside table, staring at it blindly. Oonagh had given it to her after she had learnt to read, for the dressmaker's tuition had not stopped at sewing.

Then her eyes focused on the title and she gave a laugh, sardonic humour and panic mingled in the sound.

"*Pilgrim's Progress.* Jesus, what a giggle! Harlot's Progress 'ud be more like it. God, I wish Monday were over and done with."

On the following Tuesday morning Emerald awoke from a fitful sleep. She tried to shut out of her mind what had taken place the day before but it was impossible.

She had been right about Mother Bonny. Dirty hands pawing over grimed things wrapped in a bit of cloth. Agony so excruciating that Emerald had cried out in spite of her determination not to let the old besom know how afraid she was. Nothing had happened and Mother Bonny had given her a draught. Emerald was so distraught that she wondered if Jehu had paid the woman to poison her, but in the end she had drunk it.

She had managed to get a message to Oonagh, so the latter wouldn't worry when she didn't arrive as expected.

The cart dropped her at the village inn again and Emerald had walked back to the Lodge, hardly knowing how to put one foot before the other.

She felt very sick and giddy as she got out of bed, but she had to get dressed and go to the kitchen for her usual cup of tea. Nothing must be different. She'd promised Feverell she wouldn't mention the matter and sometimes actions spoke louder than words.

She was on the stairs leading down to Mrs Duckworth's domain when the pain struck her. Blackness descended on her like a shroud, and cook, Millie and Floss turned in horror as they watched Emerald fall headlong down the steps, limp and still as she reached the bottom.

"I'll get the mistress," said Floss, shaking like a leaf. "She might be hurt bad."

"Wait." Mrs Duckworth had made a quick examination and was shaking her head. "Mistress is the last one who's to know about this."

"But why, Mrs D? We can't leave her there. What's wrong with her?"

Mrs Duckworth looked up at the two girls.

"You like Em, don't you? She's been good to the pair of you."

"'Course we like her."

"Yes, she's our friend."

"Then help her. Don't you realise what's happened?"

Millie took another look and her face whitened. She had seen such a thing before. Her own sister had lain once too often with a shepherd and got caught out by nature.

"Yes, I guess I do." She glanced at Floss, who was still bewildered. "Lost a baby, Floss, but she won't want anyone to know it. Get plenty of cloths."

"And hot water," added cook. "Then between us we'll get her up the backstairs to her room. I'll go and see missus myself. Tell her Em's got a bout of food poisoning from eating shellfish. Won't be up for a day or two, seeing how bad it's turned her stomach over."

The others nodded, rushing for the things cook needed. Em had to be protected; girls like them had to stick together when trouble came.

When Emerald woke up an hour later she was in her bed, Mrs Duckworth by her side, a glass of milk in her hand. Emerald looked at her and read the truth.

"Gone, has it?"

"Aye, lass, it's gone. Now you've got to rest."

"Can't do that. I've got to get up and ..."

"You've had too much shellfish; made you right bad, as I explained to the mistress. Very concerned she was. Told me to tell you to stay just where you are for a day or two. Here, drink this and then go to sleep."

"You helped me; you and Floss and Mill."

"You've given us all a hand in the past. We help one another."

"Think I'm awful, don't you? A proper little slut."

"I don't judge. Drink your milk."

"I didn't want to get rid of it, but there wasn't any other way."

"There never is for girls like you. Come on, luv, sup away."

Emerald obeyed, holding cook's hand for a moment.

"Won't forget this, Mrs D. Thank the others for me and ask 'em to keep mum."

She hardly saw Mrs Duckworth go. Her eyelids closed, heavy as lead, her mind mercifully blurred as she began to slip into healing slumber. She was free again, her future stretching ahead with no barriers to hold her back.

"Nicholas," She murmured the name, not knowing she'd done so as the darkness closed in. "Oh, Nicholas ....my ...love."

Emerald wasn't the only one prepared to lie with a man to get something she wanted.

Deborah Lovell was furious at Harry's continued refusal to offer for her, but it was more than pique which made her

take drastic action to remedy the situation. Her desire for
him had become a near-mania, although she still didn't
understand why. He wasn't really anything worth
bothering about, but she yearned to be his. It was just one
of those inexplicable pieces of mischief which the gods
designed now and then to torment men and women and
keep them at odds with the world.

At first she'd no idea how to bring Harry round to her
way of thinking. Sweet smiles and soft words hadn't worked
and time was passing by. Then she caught one of her
father's grooms undressing her with his eyes and that was
it. She knew then how to get her own way.

She was quite as ruthless as Emerald when she wanted
something as badly as she wanted Harry Pentreath and she
returned the man's smile in a way which he couldn't
mistake.

They met secretly, Keziah forced into helping her sister
conceal her rendezvous with James Flagg. Keziah had no
idea of the lengths to which her sister was going, but even if
she had been aware of them it was doubtful whether she
would have done anything to stop her Deb's spite, cruelty,
guile and vengefulness kept her sister in a prison without
bars. Keziah just sat in the carriage and waited for Deborah
to leave the old shack high up on the cliff.

Deborah loathed Flagg as much as Emerald had hated
Penrose and Feverell, but her will was like iron. She let the
man disrobe her, put his hands all over her body, take her
when he was ready to sate his appetite. She bore it all with
great fortitude, for at the end of the ordeal there would be
marriage with Harry.

When at last Deborah knew she was with child she told
her father. Her eyes were like saucers, full of innocent
bewilderment and fear at what had happened.

"It's his, is it?" Lovell was puce. "That swine Pentreath,
who wouldn't marry you yet had his way with you on the
sly. He'll marry you now, girl, or I'll break his neck."

"I'm sorry, Papa." Deborah shed realistic tears. "I

didn't understand what was going to happen. He was so ...so strong, you see."

"Bloody bastard! You'll be wed at once, or my name's not Edgar Lovell. Don't you cry, my sweetheart. It weren't your fault, it were his, and he's goin' to pay."

Harry listened to Lovell, his face white, seeing his father's fury turned upon him too. He refuted the accusation violently, but neither man believed him. Deborah was young and inexperienced and he'd taken advantage of her. In the end, Harry realised that it was useless. Whatever he said or did would make no difference. He was branded as a seducer and he'd have to face the consequences of that, or his father would be ruined. The only good thing which would come out of the mess was that Em would no longer be at risk. Once Deb got her way she would have no further reason to want to hurt Em.

"I'll marry her," he said, thinking of Emerald as he did so. "I've never touched Deb in my life, as God's my witness, but you'll not take my word, I sees that, so we'll be wed."

"Not before time." His father was disgusted, but relieved that Harry had at last made his promise. He'd feared a bad breach with Lovell; now perhaps things could be patched up again when the dust died down. The child, when born, might soften Edgar's present corrosive fury. "Make the arrangements, Mr. Lovell. Soon as may be, and my hand on it."

Harry walked out of the room, his stomach churning. Plump, conniving Deb was going to be his wife and he'd have to stop seeing Em once the ceremony had taken place. Deb might have dismissed Em as a threat for the moment, but if she ever found out how he felt about Tregellan's daughter there was no saying what she'd do.

He'd have to see Em to tell her what had happened. He hoped she'd understand and believe him when he told her he loved no one but her. Whether she did or not made no odds in the end. He'd lost her, and the rest of his days would be spent with Deborah and someone else's offspring.

Harry squared his shoulders, straightened up and went marching off to the village inn. There was only one way to live with his nightmare and that was to get very drunk.

"Evenin', Mr Treport," he said to the landlord. "A pint of ale, if you please; the strongest you've got. I've got a lot of drinking to do tonight and the sooner I get to it the better. Have one yourself and then pour me another. I reckon that by eight o'clock nothing much will matter to me any more.

"I've got summat to tell you, Em."

Emerald felt ill, although a week had passed since her miscarriage. In other circumstances she would have asked Ben, the stable-lad, to get word to Harry that she was off-colour and couldn't meet him that night. But the urgency of his note couldn't be ignored. Badly formed letters and atrocious spelling notwithstanding, the words had jumped off the paper at her. Something was wrong, and Harry was her friend.

"Yes?"

"Not easy to say. Don't know how to begin."

"Let's sit on that stile over there; bring the lantern. Best to see where we're putting our feet."

When Harry had got her settled she nodded encouragingly.

"Well, come on. Let's have it."

"As I said, it's hard to know how to start."

"Spit it out like a fishbone before it chokes you."

"I've got to get married."

By the light of the lantern his face looked almost ghostly.

"Got to?"

"Aye, but it ain't like it sounds. It's simply that ..."

She listened in silence, sad for him but still untouched by the thought that Harry was to take a wife. He'd told her before that it was his father's wish. She hadn't been moved by the idea then and she wasn't now.

"I'm sorry," she said at last. "If I were you I'd run away to sea. You don't love her, do you?"

"Can't abide her. You're the only one I love, but if I don't wed Deborah her father'll put mine out of business."

"Yes, I see that, but it's not fair on you."

"You do believe me, don't you?"

Her thoughts had almost drifted off. She felt weak and rather sick. Harry's problems seemed remote. She was ashamed of herself for not caring more, but she couldn't help it.

"Believe you? That her pa could ruin yours?"

"No, that I love you."

That brought her sharply back to the conversation.

"Don't love me, I'm not worth it."

"Yes, you are. I know you don't feel the same way as I do, but that don't make no difference. I'll always love you."

"Don't! For God's sake, don't."

"What's wrong?" He gave her a closer look. "You're not ill, are you? Never seen you as pale before. Got a chill, perhaps. Here, take my jersey and ..."

"Stop it!"

"I'm sorry, I just thought ..."

"No, I'm sorry. Listen, Harry, you came here to tell me something, but I've got a few things to say to you too. You won't like them, but I don't want you wasting the rest of your life pining over me. I'm no good."

"That's stupid talk. There's no better un than you. You work so hard and ..."

"Harry! Will you please listen."

She plunged straight into her confession. She knew that if she hesitated any longer she could never bring herself to tell him the truth. She kept to the bare bones, but they were sufficient.

"Oh, Em," he said when she had finished. "For money?"

"For my shop. You know I've always wanted my own place in London; I want it more than ever now. Like you said, I've worked hard and I've saved, but it isn't enough. Rents are high in the West End. Then there'd be the stock to buy, wages for the girls in the workroom, and something to live on until I got known and the orders started to come in."

"That could take years." He could see her ambition was burning as brightly as ever, unswerving and inflexible. She would always race ahead of him, even if he'd been free to ask her to be his wife. He had nothing to offer a girl like Em; he'd just be a lodestone round her neck. "When are you going?"

"Not yet; haven't got enough put by. Thought I'd start up on my own soon, here in Cornwall. Get a few clients; make 'em pay well."

"And a few more ...?"

He turned scarlet and she mocked him.

"Yes and a few more men if needs be. I don't care a button for them, but they're my ticket to success. Now do you see why you mustn't love me; why you have to forget all about me? I'm a nightingale and you know what that means."

There was silence for a while; then Harry said unhappily:

"It ought to matter, I know. I should hate you for what you've done, but I don't. I'll go on feeling about you as I do for ever. I was going to say we couldn't meet again after tonight, but I can't. Maybe we won't be able to see each other so often, but I can't face things without you."

"You'll have to." Somehow Emerald had to help Harry to say goodbye or she'd break his heart. "No use crying for what can't be."

"No!" He sounded almost angry, thrusting aside the danger of Deb's malice. "I've not had much in my life so far; there'll be even less for me in the future. Don't ask me to give you up altogether. Just to see you once or twice a year would be enough. Please, Em."

Emerald closed her eyes. She could see Nicholas Roman riding his bay, pausing by the fence at Rowett Lodge to look down at her. If she could have been sure of seeing him once or twice a year it would be enough for her, too. But she'd decided to take a different route. She couldn't have him, so she was going to put distance between them. Make a new life; become famous; reach the top and forget the agony of love. But she didn't think Harry had the same sort of iron in his soul that she had in hers.

"All right, if you want to." In the end she couldn't refuse him. "Don't let Deborah catch you or she'll make your life a misery. She sounds a proper bitch to me."

"She is, but don't worry. She won't find out. Thanks, Em."

"Wish everything could have been different."

"So do I, but not many gets what they want, do they?"

He saw her smile and was shaken by it.

"I'm going to," she said softly. "I've already paid a mighty high price and it may get higher. Nothing's going to stand in my way, not a solitary damn thing. Oh, no, Harry, nothing's going to stop me now."

"Your twenty-one, Asterly," said the earl impatiently "and Frances is seventeen. Bracknell's not going to wait for ever for you to make up your mind."

Nicholas's eyes were veiled.

Marriage with the Marquis of Bracknell's daughter, or anyone else for that matter, was so final. It would put a barrier between himself and Emily which could never be scaled. Then he gave a deep sigh. The wall was already there. She would dwell in his heart and trouble his sleep for as long as he drew breath, but he couldn't have her.

"No," he said and gave his father a quick smile. "I realise that. I suppose I ought to see Frances. I don't particularly care for the notion of offering for her sight unseen."

"We shall soon be returning to London for a month or two. You can meet her then. I'm told she's a comely wench and of amiable character."

"She sounds intolerably dull."

"Damn it, sir, are you deliberately trying to irritate me?"

"No Father, but this is my life you are trying to arrange

for me. What if I can't love Frances?"

"Very few marriages are love matches."

The viscount gave his father a straight look.

"Was yours?"

"As a matter of a fact it was." Radfield shrugged. "I was one of the lucky ones."

"But I'm not to be, is that it?"

"You won't know until you see the girl, will you?"

But the viscount did know. One couldn't love deeply as he loved his dark-haired Emily and still find any affection left over for another woman. He wondered what his father would say if he told him that he would sell his soul if he could live with a fisherman's daughter and give her his child.

Nicholas dismissed the idea, forcing himself to accept what was being thrust upon him.

"All right. Tell Bracknell I'd like to see his brat."

It satisfied the earl for the time being, but Nicholas went to the window and stared blindly at the garden. When it really came to it he doubted if he could face Frances, comely or not. But that was a problem which could wait.

Now he was going to Whitewater to see if he could catch sight of Emily. He'd ridden over there many times, but had never seen her after that first occasion.

Perhaps this would be the day and the viscount turned from the window, a smile on his lips. Maybe this would be the morning he would see Emily again.

A few weeks after meeting Harry by the stile, Emerald was feeling very low.

She had heard that he and Deborah had been married, rumour rife as to the circumstances which called for such speed. Emerald didn't think Harry would really be able to meet her, even once a year. She suspected the new Mrs Pentreath was going to keep a very close eye on her husband. The thought of not seeing Harry any more had upset her more than she had expected it to. He had been in the background for quite a time; a friend in time of need. Now she had lost him.

She was also beginning to worry about her position with the Feverells. Jehu had asked her twice already when she planned to give in her notice. She could see that he was uneasy at having her about the place, despite the promise she had given him. She sensed that if she didn't move on soon, Feverell might take steps to hasten her on her way. She was a threat to him and she doubted if he'd have any scruples when it came to protecting himself.

Every day she watched for Nicholas, but he never came. Mary and the others asked her once or twice why she kept going down to the fence which skirted the narrow lane. She had no answer for them and they had begun to look at her with curiosity.

She was trying to decide what to do as she worked on a new dress for Mary. Miss Pezzach had persuaded her some time ago to put her savings in the bank at Penzance and that she had done. She had a cheque-book which she never used, rather in awe of it, yet at the same time reassured by it because it represented security. There wasn't enough in the account yet to start up on her own, let alone take her to London, but it was a beginning.

Thinking about Oonagh made her frown. The last time she had seen her, Miss Pezzach had had a heavy cold, her chest rattling alarmingly. Emerald had tried to get her to see a physician, but Oonagh was stubborn. The cold cures handed down to her by her mother and grandmother were all she required, she had said firmly, and went about her tasks, coughing so hard that her thin body was racked to pieces.

It had filled Emerald with anxiety. Jess had coughed like that, but there hadn't been any money for a doctor. Now her sister was dead, buried in the tiny churchyard beyond the village, Daisy pressed into service in her place.

She looked up as Mrs Cheadle came into the room, getting to her feet quickly and giving a polite bob. Emerald might be a lady's maid and a fine seamstress, but the housekeeper was a tartar and very conscious of her own importance.

"There's been a message for you, Tregellan," she said, hands folded across her stomach. "Boy came over from Paul with it."

Emerald could feel her colour draining away. Whenever Mrs Cheadle took up that particular stance it meant bad news or trouble. Oonagh was the only person Emerald knew in Paul, for the Trefusis family had long since refused to acknowledge her existence.

"Yes, Mrs Cheadle?" Emerald's mouth felt dry and her heart was hammering. "What did he say?"

"Miss Pezzach has passed away. Seems she told Dr Presser to let you know if anything happened to her."

Emerald put her hand on the back of a chair to steady herself. Oonagh had called a doctor in after all, but too late. The loss of her dearest friend was bad enough, for life wouldn't be the same without her, but the greatest sadness was that she hadn't been there to say goodbye and to thank her for all she had done. If it hadn't been for Miss Pezzach she would be nothing. There would have been no future, no hope. Oonagh had given her both in abundance and love too.

After the funeral a small man, precise in manner and dress, approached Emerald.

"You are Miss Emily Tregellan?"

She didn't correct him. He didn't look the kind who'd understand why she'd changed her Christian name.

"Yes, sir."

"Then come into the house, please. I have something to tell you."

"About Miss Pezzach, do you mean? Were you the doctor who attended her?"

His smile was rusty through lack of use.

"No, I'm not a physician, I'm a lawyer. My name is Gowan, Thomas Gowan. Miss Pezzach left everything she had to you. You're her sole beneficiary and you'll be comfortably off, you'll find. Come with me and I'll explain the details. Yes, indeed, Miss Tregellan, you're a very lucky young woman."

Two months later Emerald surveyed her new home with pride. There had been a number of reasons why she'd sold Oonagh's house. First, it held too many poignant memories and secondly it was near Trefusis farm.

Oonagh had been a careful saver too, and the money she had left Emerald, together with the proceeds from the house, would have been quite sufficient for a modest start in London.

Emerald told herself she needed even more capital before she went, so that she could have things just as she wanted them when she set up her shop. It was just an excuse and she knew it.

The decision to remain in Cornwall for one more year was finally made when Emerald heard that a cottage quite close to Cloverley Park had been put up for sale. The temptation had been irresistible, and Mr Gowan had guided her through the disposal of one property and the purchase of another. The profit made from the transaction, for the cottage was smaller than Oonagh's house, enabled Emerald to call in workmen to repair and paint her new dwelling without drawing on the bank.

She threw out all the old bits of furniture, replacing them with such pieces of Oonagh's as would fit in. She had the kitchen enlarged by incorporating an outhouse, and had a Bodley Range tucked into a recess. It was a splendid fitment with a boiler on one side, an oven on the other, and an open fire between them. Its flat top accommodated kettles and saucepans and Emerald began to cook for the first time in her life. Remembering the neighbours' cottages in Porthaven, she bought a whitewood table and four chairs, a long-case clock and a dresser which she filled with colourful cups, saucers and plates. She even put a bowl of flowers in the window, where they could turn their heads to the light.

She had the two small rooms on the ground floor made into one and placed Oonagh's work-tables against the long walls. The shelves put up by the carpenter were not for useless china and knick-knacks but for bales of material, the workbox, stocks of braid, buttons and similar necessities.

However, she kept a good fire burning and the chairs pulled up to the hearth were comfortable. Everything was new and fresh and clean and it was hers.

Mrs Feverell had asked her to go on making dresses for her family; her friends had also assured Emerald that it was worth travelling a bit further to have their wardrobes made by her. Soon, others would hear about her and she would be too busy to grieve for Oonagh or long for Nicholas. However, there was a much greater chance that she might see him riding along the lanes or over the fields. Cloverley Park was only two miles away.

She would give herself twelve months to see how she got on on her own and then she'd leave Cornwall for good. She would have a healthy bank account and plenty of money in her reticule. It was a miracle, brought about by a fairy godmother and, as she sipped piping hot tea, she glanced at the miniature on the wall nearby. It was a portrait of Miss Pezzach, painted when she was a girl, young and hopeful, as Emerald was now.

Emerald had never fully expressed her gratitude to the dressmaker while the latter had lived: Miss Pezzach had always hushed her efforts and told her not to be a goose. But now the time had come to remedy the situation and Emerald gave the picture a watery smile.

"Thanks; I'm ever so grateful. I 'spect wherever you are you know that. I hope you know something else too. Maybe you guessed it before you went, but just in case you didn't I'll say it now. I loved you, dear Miss Oonagh, I really did. There won't ever be anyone else like you. You really were a good un."

FIVE

Emerald laid down her work and looked out of the window. The sun was shining, the sky a cloudless canopy of blue.

There was a lot to do, but she was her own mistress and the thought of a walk along the track at the end of her garden was too much to resist. There was always the evening to catch up with urgent jobs and often Emerald worked late into the night when she couldn't sleep. It was lonely by oneself, as Miss Pezzach had once said, and to her surprise Emerald found that she missed the family and staff at Rowett Lodge. Floss, Millie and the others had become good friends.

She took a quick look at herself in the mirror. She didn't bother with a bonnet, for no one would be about, but the muslin dress with the bishop's sleeves and long skirt flounced at the hem was good enought to wear to see the Queen, even if Emerald did say so herself.

She walked along the path for a while, a small wood on one side of her, fields on the other. She felt free and contented and in no way ready for what was about to happen.

When she saw the horseman, Emerald stopped. She had prayed for this so often, but it had never come. Now she didn't know what to do as the viscount reined to a halt and dismounted with easy grace.

As he walked over to her, Emerald felt a flicker of surprise. She hadn't realised he was so tall. She barely reached to his broad shoulders and he had a lithe strength

about him which made her quake inwardly. The first time
they had met he had been in a carriage; the second occasion
on horseback. Now he was standing close to her and it was
quite different.

At first she thought no words were going to pass between
them; that it would be as before, when they had simply
stared at each other and then the viscount had ridden away.

Afterwards, neither could remember who had moved
first. In fact, they raised their hands at precisely the same
second, Asterly closing his fingers about hers. They left the
tethered horse and began to move into the copse as if some
inner compulsion was dictating their every action. It
seemed ordained and as natural to them as breathing. It
did not strike either of them as odd that they should come
together with such passion in them, although they had only
met twice before and then in silence.

The trees and bushes closed about them and it was very
quiet. There was wonder in Emerald's eyes as lightly he
caressed her cheek.

"I love you," said Nicholas finally. "Isn't that absurd?
We have never spoken to each other before, yet you fill
every corner of my heart and mind. Since the first day I saw
you, you have been all that has mattered to me."

His voice was soft and deep, his words like a balm on a
wound.

"It's the same for me," she replied, hardly daring to
breathe in case he wasn't real but just part of another
daydream. "I've looked out for you so often."

"I rode over to Rowett Lodge many times."

"Did you? I never saw you, 'cept that one day."

"You don't work there any more?"

She blushed slightly, but it was silly to pretend she was a
grand lady when he knew quite well she wasn't.

"No. I had some money left me, so I set up in business on
my own. I'm a seamstress, you know."

"I'd been told. Where do you live now?"

"In that cottage back there. I bought it 'cos it was close

to Cloverley Park." There wasn't any point in concealing the fact now. Nicholas had said he loved her and that was what counted. "I wanted to be nearer to you."

He was sad as he took her face between his hands. They were thin and strong but very gentle.

"I can't marry you. It isn't possible."

He was arousing in her something she had never experienced before. She had felt nothing but fear with Penrose; mere disgust for Jehu Feverell. Neither had awakened her sexually, despite the fact that they had possessed her. Yet Asterly's tender gesture was like an aphrodisiac and her voice shook as she answered him.

"'Course you can't. A viscount and a fisherman's daughter! We're in different worlds, but it don't matter. I'm not worried about us being wed. Just love me, that's all I ask of you."

He felt humble in her presence. What she said was true; they were in different worlds. He wondered how a marvellous creature like her had sprung from such poverty and deprivation. Her speech betrayed her, yet it made her more endearing. She was perfect as she was; nothing needed to be changed.

He took her in his arms, knowing she must feel the violent beating of his heart. It was a moment he had waited for so long and there was no disappointment. She was all that he knew she would be, her sweet and lovely body setting his own ablaze.

He pulled her down on the grass, lips demanding, no mildness left in him. He explored her throat, lingering over its smoothness before his hand dropped to her breast. It was so different from Noah's vile abuse and she felt raw desire well up in her like a flood-tide.

Their next kiss was no polite salutation. It was fierce and wild and overwhelming as they pressed close, her arms round his neck. Their fever was mounting by the second. Each had starved for the other and now their appetite was insatiable.

"I want to hold you," he whispered, "not that fine gown you're wearing. I want to touch you and feel the warmth of you next to me."

She had undone hooks and eyes, discarding undergarments, her dress half off her shoulders when he stopped her and she could hear the torment in him.

"No! My dearest, no. I was mad to ask that of you; selfish too. You can't be my wife and I won't make a whore of you."

"I don't care." She was desperate for him to finish what he had started, her whole being aching for the final consummation. She tore the green muslin down to her waist, feeling no shame. "Don't you understand? I don't care! I need you. Oh, please don't stop; don't stop!"

The viscount closed his eyes against her beauty. She was exquisite, but she wasn't for him and slowly he leaned forward to draw up her dress to cover her nakedness.

"Do you think I want to? I have to stop, for your sake. I can't take from you what I cannot pay for. I need you too. Dear God, you'll never know how much, but I won't inflict such an injury."

Emerald's tears were beginning to dampen her lashes. It was such a rich irony yet, now it came down to it, she didn't want Nicholas to know the truth. Even to get what she craved for, she couldn't tell him she wasn't the virgin he believed her to be, but a woman already despoiled. It was a dreadful kind of game; mock theatricals in which she had to play the innocent to match his Galahad.

His eyes begged her not to torture him any longer and in the end she gave in.

"All right, but whenever you want me I'm yours. Don't care a damn for what's proper. I just want to belong to you."

"You should care, my darling, I do. One day you'll find a man to marry; a man to give you children. You must wait for him and I mustn't steal what should be his."

Her cheeks were wet and a smile wouldn't come no

matter how hard she tried to muster her courage.

"There'll never be no one but you, you know that. If you won't make love to me, kiss me once more as you did just now. Don't tease me with a peck; kiss me hard so as I'll remember it. Give me that, at least, if nothin' else."

He held her tightly to him, hurting her with the savagery of his despair, yet her heart was singing until he released her. Then the paradise she'd been in vanished. She was sitting on the grass in a small wood, everyday sights all around her.

"Oh, my love," he said quietly, "why were we put on this earth at the same time and in the same place if we cannot have each other? Truly the gods are cruel and my life is going to be so empty without you."

"I shan't give up hope."

"You must!"

"I won't; not ever."

"It will make your existence a misery."

"Better to feel misery than nothin' at all."

"Dear God!"

He held her hand briefly. Then he rose quickly, striding away to the lane and out of her sight.

Emerald didn't move for a while. She lay back and watched the sun send gilded shafts of light through the leaves. She hadn't expected to meet Nicholas, that day or any other. Now she had lain in his arms, but he had said it was finished. She relived the precious interlude, knowing she'd do so many times, touching her lips where he had bruised them. Love like theirs was not a kind and peaceful thing.

If she had told him the real facts about herself she might be his by now. More likely, however, he would have walked away from her in disgust. What she had concealed had kept his love alive; he would remember her in the way he wanted to and perhaps that might bring him some consolation.

And no one knew what the future would bring. She got up and brushed her skirt, fastening the bodice of her dress.

The gods might be cruel, but they couldn't be as vicious as all that. If she was to survive, she had to believe what her heart was telling her.

One day she would see Nicholas again; one day she really would be his.

The next day Viscount Asterly left Cornwall. Some rumours claimed he'd gone to France, other said to Italy. The only thing the gossip-mongers agreed about was that the earl was furious. He'd wanted his son to marry a marquis's daughter, but that was all over now. The girl was going to be the wife of a duke's heir instead.

Emerald knew why Nicholas had gone but she still wept. France or Italy, it made no difference. He was a very long way away. She accepted more and more orders, glad to be on the point of exhaustion when night came. Sleep was more healing than memories. She was like one of the outdoor workers Oonagh had told her about; slaving away to produce gowns for rich, impatient women. Only the motive was different.

When the year she had set herself was up, she had had enough. Harry had left an address where she could write to him without Deborah finding out and she let him know of her proposed departure. He came within a day or two, flushing askwardly as she kissed him soundly and gave him a hug.

"It's good to see you, Harry; I've missed you."

"I've missed you too, Em. Do you have to go to London? It's so far off."

He saw the shadow across her eyes, wishing he could find the right words to deal with her sorrow.

"What is it? Summat amiss?"

She gave him a quick smile.

"No, just that there are places a good deal further off than London."

"Suppose so. Are you happy, Em?"

She was glad she was pouring the tea, for it gave her a

chance to bend her head over the cups. Sometimes Harry could be quite perceptive.

"Happy enough. What about you? Getting on all right with Deborah, are you? Is she better tempered now she's got you to cuddle up to?"

When he didn't reply she looked up.

"Harry? Did I say the wrong thing?"

"You weren't to know."

"Know what?"

"She don't cuddle up to me, never has. Can't abide me near her."

Emerald stared at him.

"That don't make sense, not after what she did to get you."

"Think that's what did it. After we were wed, on the first night, she cried out when I went to ...to ...well, you know. I was trying to make the best of it, but she wouldn't 'ave it. Then she told me just what she'd done to get herself with child. At the time, she said it didn't seem so bad. It were afterwards that she realised she'd never be able to let another man touch her, not even me. God punished her right enough, for she did want me. I think she still loves me, in her own way, but she can't show it no more."

"And the baby?"

"She's a pretty thing. If it weren't for her, I don't know what Deb would be like. Susan's everything to her."

"It's rotten for you."

He shrugged.

"We rub along. She looks after me well, I'll say that for her. She's a good cook and I'm never short of a clean shirt come Sunday. It's just that she hates lovemaking now."

"Do you hate lovemaking, Harry?" Emerald asked very softly, trying to conceal her pity, for he wouldn't thank her for that. "How do you feel about it?"

He avoided her eye, colouring up again.

"I'd like it fine with the right woman."

"You've never asked me to sleep with you. Why not?"

"'Cos I love you. Wouldn't be right."

"Perhaps not. In any event, I don't reckon I'll be bedding down with any man again."

Then he did glance at her and saw her hands were gripped tightly together.

"You haven't ...?"

"No, I haven't, not since Jehu Feverell."

"I'm glad."

"Don't think I've become an angel just because no one shares my pillow. You see, there's a man ..."

He tried not to care, but she could see it still mattered to him.

"Don't look like that. He's not my lover; don't suppose he ever will be. Things aren't likely to work out for us."

"Where is he now?"

"Abroad."

"A good deal further off than London, eh? I'm sorry, Em, I know how it feels."

"Yes you do, don't you, luv. Well, never mind. We've both got problems but we don't have to cry into our tea, do we?"

"Will I ever see you again, Em?"

"If you come to London you will."

"You won't be coming back here?"

She didn't answer for a long time. Then she said very quietly:

"No, I won't return to Cornwall no more."

"Will he, do you think?"

"Certain to."

"Then why ...?"

"Because it would tear him to bits. He can't marry me and he won't let me be his mistress. I'd be glad enough to lie with him on any terms, but he's like you."

"Like me?"

"Yes, he loves me and he's an honourable man. Too many scruples, the pair of you." She pushed her heartache aside; it wasn't fair to burden Harry with it. "So I'm off to seek fame and fortune. Wish me luck."

While she was speaking, Harry had been trying to guess
who the man was. Someone honourable and who was now
abroad. Things began to come together in his mind but he
stifled them. It wasn't his business.

"I do, Em, I do. Write to me now and then if you've got
the time."

"I'll always find time for you. You know how fond I am
of you."

"But you love him."

It wasn't a question but she answered it anyway, her eyes
blinded by tears.

"Yes and I'll go on loving him until I die. Women are
fools when they lose their hearts, and I'm the biggest fool of
the lot. Oh, Harry, put your arms round me. I feel so
bloody miserable."

Emerald found a house on the edge of Bloomsbury. It was a
narrow slip of a place but its situation was good enough for
the time being and easy of access to Regent Street, Oxford
Street and Bond Street.

Emerald had sold her cottage as it stood, bringing no
furniture with her. She was sure Oonagh would have
understood. It had to be a completely new beginning, with
nothing to reflect the past.

Fortunately, her London home was a pleasant one. It
belonged to an earlier era; pastel-coloured walls, graceful
tables and chairs and everything spick and span.

She took over the servants with the house: Mrs Grisdale,
the cook; Stegall, the maid, and an undernourished boy of
about twelve called Bert Clemson.

"'E sleeps in the stables at the back, ma'm," said Mrs
Grisdale, fat and rosy-cheeked. "'E don't eat much, but you
can get rid of 'im if you want to. 'E just cleans boots and
runs errands and such."

Emerald saw the hopelessness in Bert's eyes. Clearly he
didn't expect to be kept on and the scraps which had

sustained him for the last year or two would soon dry up as
he slid into starvation.

"'Course I'll keep him," she said shortly, "but if he
doesn't get three square meals a day from now on, I'll want
to know the reason why."

Cook bridled, recognising the criticism, but Emerald had
gone on to study Stegall. Miss Pezzach had once told
Emerald that when she finally got to London she mustn't
go out and about unchaperoned. "It simply isn't done," the
dressmaker had said. "You must find yourself a lady's maid
or a companion."

Stegall was stolid, plain and with a rash of spots on her
face. She looked sulky and Emerald knew she would never
take to the girl. However, she would have to do until other
arrangements could be made. She wasn't going to postpone
her exploration of the shops and sights of town just because
the maid wasn't an ideal chaperon.

Fortunately, Stegall's role as a duenna was short-lived.
On the second day in town, Emerald ventured into
Tottenham Court Road, the maid a pace or two behind
her, grumbling to herself about the extra work and her
corns.

When Emerald saw the violet-seller she stopped,
reaching into her reticule for some coins. The old woman
with the basket wore a linsey-woolsey gown, open in front
to show her red petticoat, with a mob-cap topped by an
ancient straw hat. There were gay ribbons fluttering from it
and her toothless but infectious grin somehow made
Emerald feel at home. Not everyone was grand in London
town and she paid twice the value of the flowers, returning
the smile.

She wasn't even aware that she had dropped a coin until
she heard a quiet voice at her elbow.

"Forgive me, madam. This is yours."

Emerald looked first at the penny and then at the woman
who had picked it up. It was obvious that she was very
poor. Her dress was thin and well darned, her shawl no

better. The bonnet she wore was limp and battered, her feet visible through the holes in her scuffed shoes.

But Emerald looked beyond the rags. The woman's face was a perfect oval, the cheeks sunken now through lack of sustenance. The eyes were dark, underlined by the marks of fatigue and filled with something which reminded Emerald of a wounded animal.

"Thank you. What's your name?"

"Verity Dean."

"Well, Verity Dean, you could have bought yourself a meat pie or such like with this. Why didn't you?"

"Because the penny isn't mine. If I'd kept it, it would have been theft."

Verity wasn't offended. She'd grown used to people's harsh comments and assumptions since she'd lost her job a year before. One had to grow a thick skin or bleed to death.

"Sorry." Emerald gave Verity a warm smile. "That wasn't a nice thing to ask, was it? But you see I've been poor like you. I've worn rags worse than you've got on and I know what it means to long for food so much you'd almost kill to get it."

"You, madam?"

Emerald was wry. She could understand the disbelief, for her gown was of best quality silk, as fashionable as anything Paris could offer. She had trimmed the fetching bonnet herself and she was using some of Harry's illicit perfume.

"Yes, me. Got a job, have you?"

"I did have one, but I fell ill and the family wouldn't wait. They found a new governess."

"Ah, governess, were you? That's just what I need. How would you feel about working for me? I need a companion and a teacher, who can also be a lady's maid. Think you could manage all that?"

"I'm sure I couldn't. A lady like you would want someone far more efficient than I."

"But I'm not a lady and you are; that's the whole point.

I'll give you a room of your own, as much food as you can eat, decent clothes to wear and thirty pounds a year. What do you say?"

"That I'm not qualified for what you want."

"Do you know which knife to use first at table and how to address people of quality?"

Verity hesitated.

"Yes, but ..."

"Then you're qualified. I've got to learn all those things and how to speak like you do. When we've got you put to rights, I'll tell you why it's so important to me."

"I could manage those things, but I wouldn't know how to care for such beautiful clothes as you're wearing. Please don't think I'm impertinent, but did that outfit come from France?"

"The silk did, smuggled in by a friend of mine. I made the dress myself. I've got a roomful more at home and soon I'll have a shop full of 'em. Still, all that can wait. I'll show you how to handle materials, don't fret about that. Can you do the rest?"

"I ...yes, I think so."

"Then you're hired."

"Madam, why are you helping me like this? You could get far better services than mine for such remuneration."

Emerald didn't answer at once. When she did speak, Verity could see the sadness in her.

"Because when I was like you, only much younger, a woman helped me. It wasn't only a meal and a warm petticoat she gave me, but a future which was worth living. She was a seamstress and she taught me all I know. She gave me another thing I'd never had until then; she gave me love. When she died, she left me her money. That's why I'm here. Oh, one more thing before you make up your mind."

Emerald turned to Stegall, shuffling her feet and looking disagreeable. She couldn't catch everything her mistress had said, but she didn't like the look of the vagrant Miss

Tregellan was talking to.

"Stegall, go on ahead. Tell Mrs Grisdale to get a hot meal going and be quick about it."

She watched the maid go, then frowned.

"I don't like telling you this, but before you come under my roof there's something you ought to know about me. It's only fair to you."

"Yes? What is that?"

Emerald told Verity briefly but succinctly about Noah Penrose and Jehu Feverell, holding nothing back.

"Does it make a difference?" Emerald felt a strange anxiety, for she had taken an immediate liking to Verity Dean. "I'm what's called a fallen woman. If you feel you can't help me, I'll understand."

Verity was reassuring.

"On the first occasion you were assaulted. The second time you had to agree or lose your position. No one could blame you for what you did, that is, no one who knows what it's like to be without a home, food or money."

"There was another reason the second time. Perhaps I'll tell you about it one day when we know one another a bit better. I'm glad it makes no odds. I think I need you more than you need me, so don't you worry yourself about giving value. Now let's be off, it's time you had a bite to eat."

Two months later Emerald sat down to consider all that she had seen, and to think about where her own shop should be.

There had been some changes in her household in the preceding eight weeks. Verity Dean had slipped into her role with surprising ease. Food, rest, new clothes and, most of all, kindness had made a different woman of her.

She had proved a very stern tutor, correcting Emerald's grammatical lapses, improving her spelling and writing, teaching her table manners and other social graces and even how to dance the Quadrille and Galop. When she had

heard what Emerald's goal was she had seen at once the
necessity for such strictness and had given her pupil no
quarter.

Stegall had been replaced by a cheerful girl called
Maisie, and Bert, his colour restored and some flesh on his
bones, had become Emerald's adoring slave.

It had been an exhausting time, too. Every day Emerald
had sallied forth with Verity to see what the London shops
had to offer. She was overcome by the splendour of Nash's
Regent Street, particularly the Quadrant, visiting Swan
and Edgar, linen drapers; Mrs Elizabeth Fox and Son,
wool and silk mercers; Miss Clarke, who specialised in
antique lace, and Dickins, Smith and Stevens, where she
acquired tiffanies, some fancy handkerchiefs and half a
dozen worked muslin trimmings. Jn. & J. Holmes sold only
shawls and Verity almost cried when Emerald had
presented her with one of the most expensive on show.

She got two prints from Ackermann's for the dining-
room, and from Wheeler and Company some elegant
French gloves. The tiny parasols with folding ivory sticks
and thick silk fringes weakened her resistance as she bought
three of different colours. She purchased sweetmeats from
Charles Verry for Maisie, cook and Bert; spent hours in the
Royal Opera Arcade and Burlington Arcade, dazzled by
the luxurious wares on display in the bijou shops. Her only
sadness was that she knew of no child for whom she could
buy a toy from Morel's, whose captivating stock included
dolls' houses, miniature furniture and tiny animals made of
wood, china and glass.

Bond Street was her next port of call and while Verity
browsed in the bookshops, Emerald's eye fell upon Savory
and Moore's. Although many of the grander shops now had
plate-glass, the chemist's living quarters still retained small
panes with a curtain for privacy. Below, there were carboys
full of brightly coloured water, and inside the shop there
was a heady smell of soap, herbs, oils and aromatic

specifics. Emerald spent so freely there, humbly impressed
by the fact that the Duke of Wellington was a customer,
that she was allowed to see the dispensers at work and even
take a peep into the cellars, where drums of turpentine,
white lead, castor oil, sulphur, camphor and many other
goods were stored.

Oxford Street, considered to be Regent Street's poor
cousin, was nevertheless of great interest because it
specialised in fashion. Emerald walked its length two or
three times, pausing to visit Peter Robinson's to buy some
bed linen, caps for cook and Maisie, and a box of French
beads.

But the West End was not the only place which had to be
investigated.

It wasn't only Fortnum and Mason's delicacies which
Emerald wanted to taste. She dragged her companion off to
Hungerford Market and that in New Cut, Lambeth,
giggling as she offered Verity the choice of a ha'porth of
sweets or a bag of hot chestnuts.

They admired the pictures in the National Gallery; had a
meal in a small restaurant in Soho; sighed over the superior
shops in Tottenham Court Road and took hansom cabs
home at the end of the day when they were too tired and
laden to walk another step.

"Well," said Emerald one evening. "It's clear there
aren't many really high-class or court dressmakers about.
There's Mrs Bell, of course. Now she's the one I must
follow. I'm told she employs only the best seamstresses in
her place in St James's and she had the sense to marry a
publisher. I've read her magazine *The Court Magazine and
Belle Assemblée*. Did I pronounce that right?"

"You pronounced it correctly." Verity was tired but
something about Emerald kept her going. Her mistress was
so full of life and high spirits that it was impossible to feel
flat in her company. "What are we going to do next? Don't
you think you should rest for a while?"

"Wearing you out, am I?" Emerald laughed. "No, I've no time to rest, but I'll take Maisie with me tomorrow, if you like."

"Of course not." Verity dismissed the idea at once. "I'm strong; it was you I was thinking of."

Emerald's smile faded.

"I'm strong too; I've had to be. I want to see the cheaper kind of shops next. I don't want to miss anything, not even the Rag Fair near the Tower."

But Emerald's frenetic tour was coming to an end, although she didn't realise it when she went to bed that night.

On the following morning she and Verity set out to find one of those places where, so a scornful Oxford Street salesman had told her, they marked the goods with a price tag in their windows. It seemed a further warning was given to would-be buyers; a notice to the effect that there would be no abatement, or lower price, in view of the exceptional bargains being offered.

"I'm sure that madam wouldn't care for them," the man had said as he wrapped Emerald's purchases. "They sacrifice the goodwill of regular customers and a decent profit, simply to get a quick turnover."

Emerald looked as chic as any of Mrs Bell's fashion-plates. Her gown of pink grenadine had tight sleeves ending in a small frill, the wide skirt trimmed 'en tablier'. The bonnet was adorned with rose-coloured ribbon and tulle and she wore a pair of scented gloves, carrying one of the parasols she had bought a week before.

They went into the first shop they encountered which had its goods marked and extolled by hand-written signs. Emerald was examining some blue taffeta when she became aware that she was being carefully observed. She turned her head and saw a smartly dressed man at her elbow.

He was of medium height, well built, with a ready smile and humorous eyes. Emerald considered the jaunty angle of his tall hat over sandy curls; whiskers, neatly cropped, coming down each side of his face. She rather liked the look of him and, to Verity's consternation, gave him a broad smile.

He doffed his hat at once, bowing politely.

"Does it meet with your approval?"

"This?" Emerald ran a contemptuous hand over the bale of material. "It's rubbish. Not worth putting a needle into it. Whoever owns this shop ought to be ashamed of himself."

His laugh was totally disarming.

"I'm afraid it belongs to me," he admitted without contrition. "I've got others, but this one caters for people without much cash."

"You have other shops?" Emerald's interest was caught and held. "Where? Have you got an establishment like Mrs Bell's or Madame Dumany's?"

"Dear me, no; too rich for my blood. I've got a place in Oxford Street, another near St Paul's Churchyard and a stall in Soho Market."

"You ought to aim higher. Just look at that stuff over there. Might almost have been dropped in a bucket of water."

He chuckled again.

"Not dropped in, just dipped. We couldn't move it at its original price, so we gave it a bit of a dousing, knocked off a few pence, and are selling it as salvage stock. Of course, I don't do that sort of thing in my manufactory in the City, or the warehouse in Oxford Street."

"What's the difference between a manufactory and a warehouse?"

"The first is where all the goods sold are made on the premises. The other sells things made by other workrooms. By the way, my name's Eugene Ryan."

"I'm Emerald Tregellan and this is my companion, Miss Dean. When I open my salon I intend to call myself Madame Virot, for it's to be a most exclusive place and a French name is quite essential, don't you agree?"

"Indubitably." His lips twitched. He thought she was the most delightful creature he'd seen in many a long day and he wanted to keep her talking in spite of her chaperon's censorious looks. "Where and when are you going into business?"

"I'm not sure yet." Emerald gave Eugene an appraising look. He was personable, clearly well-off and with plenty of experience in business, and a thought had suddenly struck her. "Tell me, Mr Ryan, what do you think of the outfit I'm wearing?"

"It is one worthy of a goddess, such as you," he replied gallantly. "It is perfection and ..."

"I'm not asking for compliments; that's not my way. Look at the gown itself. You're in the garment business. What do you make of it.?"

He looked at it more closely and shook his head.

"I'm not in that kind of garment business, Miss Tregellan. That's a French model, isn't it?"

Her smile was slow and satisfied.

"I'm glad you think so. The grenadine cost three pounds. I got it cheap because I told the man it was flawed. It wasn't, but I'm a good fibber."

Eugene's eyes narrowed.

"Three pounds? But who made it?"

"I did."

He was dumbfounded and it was her turn to laugh.

"Come home with me and I'll show you more of my work. I've got two roomfuls of gowns and mantles there."

He had started to frown.

"I don't disbelieve you, but why do you want me to see them? I'm overcome with admiration, of course, but ..."

"I want you to take a good look at them and then decide whether you'd like to go into partnership with me. Not in a place like this." She waved a dismissive hand round Eugene's cut-price store. "Somewhere where only the very wealthy buy their clothes."

"A partnership? My dear Miss Tregellan, you don't waste much time, do you? We've only been talking to each other for about ten minutes. You don't know anything about me, nor I a thing about you."

"I'll put the last bit right here and now." Emerald ignored Verity's gasp. She was certain her judgment about Eugene Ryan was sound and she wasn't going to let such a chance slip by. If he turned her down in the end, nothing would have been lost, but somehow she didn't think he would. "You want to know about me ..well ...here goes."

She was very blunt, as she had been with Verity. What she had hidden from Nicholas she told Eugene without a second thought.

"Yes, I sold my body to get money. I'd have done it again and again if I hadn't had that legacy." She refused to listen to the small inner voice which was calling her a liar. After Nicholas's kiss, she couldn't have done it even once more. "Well, does that shock you?"

Eugene was just getting his breath back. He had merely come into the shop that morning to see if all was well and whether the goods were moving reasonably fast. It was true that he'd spoken to Miss Tregellan first, but he hadn't expected a frank, unexpurgated version of her life story, nor the suggestion of a partnership.

"No," he said eventually, "it doesn't shock me, but it frightens me. I don't think I've got your sort of courage. My father left me my shops. I didn't have to work for them or pay any other kind of price. As to going into business with you, well I'd have to think hard about that. You're completely unknown and it would be my capital."

"Half would be yours, the other half mine. I'd look after the workshop, the girls, and the making of the clothes. I'd sell them too, but only to the rich and famous, and perhaps royalty as well."

"You've got plenty of self-confidence, I'll say that for you." Ryan pursed his lips. At first he'd rejected the idea as

ridiculous, but for some reason he was now beginning to
warm to it. "What do you want from me, other than my
money?"

"You know a lot about the trade at all levels, even if you
do sell muck like this." Her smile took the sting out of the
words. "Don't worry; you'd be useful. Well, are you
coming home to look at my stuff or aren't you?"

Over luncheon, Eugene continued to ponder. The girl's
work was better than anything he'd ever seen. Women
would go wild for what Miss Tregellan's slim fingers could
coax out of a length of satin or velvet, but there was still a
risk.

"Tell you what," he said finally. "I know a woman who's
got a place not far from here. She wants to sell. We'll go and
see her some time, shall we?"

"Wrong area. I want a better address."

"Start modestly. If you make your name, you can pick
your spot. We'll get this particular business cheap, and if
things don't work out the loss won't be so high for either of
us."

The green eyes met his, red lips curving up at the
corners.

"I'll make my name, Mr. Ryan, don't you worry about
that, and there's not going to be any losses either. Still, I've
got a bit to learn about how things are done in London and,
as you say, we can always move. In about six months or so,
I'd say."

Eugene's frame shook with suppressed laughter. He
found Emerald utterly fascinating. Strangely, she didn't
arouse in him even a flicker of sexual desire; he had Tess,
Mabel and the others when he felt like a romp. It was quite
a different feeling that Miss Tregellan stirred in him. A
sense of being carried along on the crest of a wave and a
successful wave at that. She was not only extraordinarily
gifted, she had such vivacity and a sense of purpose which
he knew nothing would deflect. As she had proved, she
would stop at nothing to achieve her ends; she would get to

the top whatever it cost. She was beautiful and ambitious and he had no defences against her. He supposed he was lucky that he'd met her first; there were a number of men of his acquaintance who would have jumped at the opportunity of going into business with Emerald. Even the fancy name she'd chosen for herself suited her.

"All right, six months. When do you want to see the place I was talking about?"

Emerald laid aside her napkin and stood up.

"Straight away," she said without hesitation. "Nothing like the present, is there? You might have gone off the idea by tomorrow."

He rose too, his amusement growing.

"I doubt it. Maybe I'm mad; who knows? Yet something tells me you'll get what you want. When you do I shall make a tidy sum by simply sitting back and watching you."

"Is it a bargain, then?"

He took her hand and kissed it ceremoniously.

"It's a bargain, Madame Virot, and we'll have the papers drawn up tomorrow. Meanwhile, come and have a look at your new premises. Do you know, I think you're just about to start making our fortunes."

Emerald gave a mock curtsy.

"You just think I am, Mr. Ryan. I know I am. Come on, let's go and get on with it, shall we?"

SIX

Nine months later Emerald had the shop of her dreams. A combination of Eugene's business acumen, Emerald's skill, and a piece of luck had achieved her life-long ambition. She had also bought herself a very desirable residence in Court Street.

She had been in a very exclusive shop in Regent Street, buying yet another parasol, when a stout woman approached her, gimlet eyes running over Emerald's gown of lilac taffeta.

"Don't know you," the woman had said abruptly, "but that can't be helped. Who dresses you, my gel?"

Emerald had hesitated but only for a second. No one but the excessively wealthy or those of high birth broke society's rules so casually.

"I dress myself." Emerald had felt a quickening of the pulse. "I might dress you too, if you give me a free hand. I don't want your advice or suggestions, just your measurements."

The woman had cackled with laughter, ignoring the looks of frozen horror on the faces of the assistants standing by.

"God's teeth, so you shall, you young minx. I like you. Come and see me tomorrow at ten and make sure you don't keep me waiting."

"I might come." Emerald's attention had wandered back to the parasols, pretending that every nerve in her body wasn't quivering with excitement. "I'll see how I feel. Who are you and where do you live, just in case I decide I'll call on you?"

"I'm the Duchess of Lammerton and my house is in Grosvenor Square. You be there at the time I've told you or you can go to hell. If you come, I'll make all London ring with your name."

The duchess and Emerald soon became good friends. Her Grace was both affluent and extremely influential, if a trifle unconventional, and she kept her promise. Within a few months everyone who was anyone wanted Madame Virot to make their gowns for them. Now and then Emerald would visit her clients; mostly she made them come to her and they adored her for it.

Her salon was in exactly the right place, a tiny brass plate announcing her name but nothing else.

"If they don't know what I do, they're not worth bothering with," she had said to the admiring Eugene as she gave orders for a single pelerine to be placed in the window next to a red rose made of silk. "Now, Eugene, about improving the girls' accommodation ..."

Emerald had kept in touch with Harry. In her last two letters to him she had asked, as off-handedly as she could, how the earl and countess were and whether the viscount had returned to England.

Harry wasn't surprised. He had guessed the name of the man whom Emerald loved and grieved for her. Asterly was far out of her reach.

But one day he met Nicholas Roman and quite suddenly he knew what he had to do for Em. It would be the last gift he'd give her, for he wouldn't see her again.

"Do you remember me, m'lord?"

Asterly had an excellent memory for those who lived in the villages around Cloverley Park, even if he sometimes forgot the identity of the eager belles who sought to lure him into their beds.

"Of course. You're Harry Pentreath, aren't you? Still free trading?"

Harry shuffled his feet in embarrassment, but Nicholas laughed.

"That wasn't a criticism, m'dear fellow. Your last consignment of cognac was quite excellent."

"Thank you, sir. I'm glad it satisfied. I wanted to tell you ..."

"Yes?"

Harry gulped, cheeks like fire, wishing he'd never started the conversation.

"It would be an impertinence."

"Only if I say so." Nicholas was thoughtful. McFee had discovered that Pentreath was a friend of Emily Tregellan's. He knew he ought to have ended the discussion there and then, but he couldn't. It was a weakness, and he recognised that, but his feeling for Emily had never wavered. He might have acted honourably on the last occasion they had met, but he had also been a fool. She had wanted him so much that it had brought her nothing but pain when he had walked away. He should have loved her as she had wanted him to and forgotten his scruples. "What did you want to tell me?"

"It were nothing."

"Tell me."

Harry looked up and saw the viscount's face had hardened. His lordship had guessed what it was about and he wasn't going to be put off.

"I had a letter from Em," said Harry, knowing there was no escape. He didn't bother to give her surname either, for the viscount knew well enough whom he meant. "She's got a new house now; sounds like a palace. She asked after you."

"I'm going to London with my parents soon. Give me her address."

"Well ... I ..."

"Please!"

The urgency in Asterly's voice made Harry twitch.

"You won't hurt her, sir, will you?"

"Probably." Nicholas's voice was clipped. "Just as she'll hurt me. It doesn't make any difference. Do you understand what I'm talking about?"

After a long while, Harry sighed.

"Aye, reckon I do."

Just for a moment the viscount and the free trader were men on equal terms.

"Did you love her too, Harry?"

"Still do."

"I'm sorry."

"Can't be helped; you're the one she wants."

"I know; I want her too."

"Life's not easy, is it?"

"It's bloody hard. That's why we should snatch at happiness when we can. I let it slip through my fingers once before. I shan't do that again. For her sake, if not for mine, tell me where she lives. Let Em be happy too, if only for a short while. We'll soon be dead, the whole lot of us."

When Emerald got Harry's next letter she was filled with a joy which seemed to light up the morning.

"Verity, he's coming to London! Do you hear? Nicholas is coming up to town very soon."

Verity, who had listened sympathetically to Emerald's tale of the man she loved but couldn't have, felt a twinge of fear.

"Will you see him, do you think?"

"I hope so; oh God, I hope so. He asked Harry for my address. He wouldn't have done that unless he meant to call on me at Court Street, would he?"

"Is he married?"

Verity didn't want to spoil her mistress's happiness but she had to make her face realities.

"I don't know and I don't care." Emerald picked up a half-finished sleeve and held it against her cheek as if she were caressing Nicholas himself. "All that matters is that he's coming. He can have six wives and a dozen children; I don't care a damn. I'm going to see him again. Oh, Verity, isn't everything wonderful!''

"Mother, do I really have to come to this place with you? Surely Matilde or Sophie could accompany you."

Juliet Roman sipped her breakfast coffee and smiled at Nicholas. He recognised the smile at once. It was the same kind which she used to bestow on him when he was a child. It was a signal that whatever he said or did she was going to have her own way.

Juliet was bothered about her son, although no one looking at her would have guessed it. She hadn't even mentioned her fears to Selwyn, for she had insufficient evidence at present to put a case before him. In any event, he did fuss so.

Her concern had its roots in the subdued but evident happiness which the viscount had displayed for the past week. His contentment had manifested itself in odd ways: a snatch of a song when he thought no one was about his lack of ennui, his willingness to stay at home and dine with his parents instead of seeking his normal company, and a look in his eyes which the countess understood only too well.

Nicholas was in love. Usually Juliet found nothing alarming about such a state of affairs, for normal, healthy young men were prone to such malaise. Her doubts were as to the identity of the woman. Nicholas's suppressed elation had started when they were still at Cloverley Park, but it had not faded now they had reached London. She didn't know whether his amie was in Cornwall or the capital. The only thing she was certain about was that it had nothing to do with the latest girl the earl wanted Nicholas to marry.

"They could, my dear, but they're not going to. You are. Lady Levett tells me that everyone these days is going to Madame Virot for their clothes. They are the *dernier cri*, and you don't want your mother to be the only woman in society to look a frump, do you?"

"No, sweet, I just don't like shopping."

"Visiting Madame Virot's is scarcely shopping. It is an

experience which no one should miss, or so all my acquaintances tell me."

"I think I should survive the lack of it."

"Don't be aggravating, dear. You're coming with me unless, of course, you have something else of greater importance to do. Have you, Nicholas?"

The viscount grew wary. It was clear that his mother had already seen too much for his peace of mind. He would have to stop thinking about Em or he would give himself away. He was no match for the countess and he knew it.

"No, nothing. Very well, I'll come with you if it will please you."

"I felt sure you would." Juliet patted his hand, but the glint in her eyes did nothing to allay his fears. "It won't be nearly as bad as you think."

The viscount gave an inward sigh. His mother's tactics were clear. She had noticed the difference in him and she was going to keep him on a short leash. Getting to see Em would require careful planning, cunning strategy and a considerable amount of luck.

The temple of fashion owned by Madame Virot met with the countess's approval as soon as they crossed the threshold. The carpet was pearl grey, the drapes a deeper shade tied back with cerise bands. There were gilt-framed mirrors on the walls, faint perfume in the air, delicately wrought chairs for favoured clients to sit on and charming, subservient *vendeuses* in black silk gliding forward to bob their welcome.

The madness of the 1830's was over. Huge sleeves had collapsed; ludicrously decorated hats were *démodé*; exuberance was dead. In its place had come modesty, humility, helplessness and fragility.

Hair was now smoothed down and braided in loops over the ears; bonnets shielded blushing cheeks; arms were kept still by the dropped shoulder-line of the gown; the bodice was longer, neater and adhering rigidly to the tightly laced corset. Skirts were full, petticoat upon petticoat used to increase their width. It was the thing nowadays to be pale and languid, as if afflicted by some terminal illness. Woman had to be cherished and protected by man, and her appearance never let him forget it.

While they waited for Madame Virot to appear, the countess drew Nicholas's attention to some gowns the girls were showing to another visitor.

"How splendid," she whispered. "Do you think I would look well in that scarlet velvet? It is so lavishly embroidered, so opulent. But perhaps I would be at my best in the pink watered-silk, or even that marvellous cream-coloured dress covered with lace. Lettice Levett was right; I wouldn't have missed this for anything. Madame Virot's designs are better than any Parisian's. Oh, I think I shall have the pink and the red, unless that dreadful woman is going to buy them. She is far too fat to carry off either of them. I really think the *vendeuses* should tell her so; it would be a kindness. Ah, here is Madame Virot, I fancy."

Nicholas's attention had been straying, but when he glanced up he felt as though the ground had moved under his feet.

Emerald advanced slowly and gracefully, her dark hair drawn back into a knot, her gown deep crimson against pearl-white flesh. For a moment the viscount thought she looked like a madonna; then he changed his mind. She was seduction itself; Delilah, Eve and Lilith rolled into one and he was a man stumbling about in a nightmare. He prayed that his mother wouldn't recognise her. Then his heart slowed down to a normal beat again. Juliet hadn't seen the shabby child standing by their carriage that day; she had said so. Besides, no one looking at Em now would connect her with that urchin.

"You are most welcome, my lady." Emerald's voice was soft and well modulated. "I am honoured by your visit."

Nicholas missed her West Country accent and rough grammar. It felt as though part of her had slipped away from him. He had gathered from Harry Pentreath that

Emily was doing well, but the possibility that she was the
famous Madame Virot had never crossed his mind.

"This is my son," said Juliet, disposed to be gracious, for
she could see that Madame was going to be a considerable
asset to her. "Viscount Asterly."

"My lord." Emerald met his eyes without blinking,
although how she managed it she had no idea. She wanted
to throw herself into his arms and kiss him, but all she did
was to incline her head. "How wise of the countess to bring
a discerning man with her."

Juliet gave Emerald a harder look. There was something
in her she hadn't quite expected. Too much self-possession
and a touch of arrogance, but nowadays these fashionable
dressmakers did give themselves airs and graces and one
had to endure such things if one were to outvie one's
contemporaries.

"I was looking at that pink silk," said the countess,
dismissing her faint irritation. "And the scarlet velvet is
quite enchanting. They are far ahead of French styles.
Would they suit me, do you think?"

"No." Emerald was uncompromising. "They are not
subtle enough for you. Your gowns must be specially
designed to heighten the mystery in you. Your attire has to
be as enigmatic as you are. To aim for less would be to
cheat nature."

Nicholas could hardly believe his ears, but his mother
was purring.

"How very perceptive you are, madame. So few
dressmakers in the past have understood that, but you saw
it straight away."

"Yes, but I'm not a dressmaker; I'm an artist. I use
women on whom to paint my masterpieces, not canvas.
Cecile, take her ladyship into the Blue Room. I want to
show her some very rare fabrics which have just arrived
from Paris."

The countess went like a lamb and Nicholas said softly:

"Good God, what has happened to you?"

Emerald gave a quick grin, looking like the girl of long ago.

"I got myself a tutor, a partner, and a fortune, in that order. Oh, my love, it is so good to see you."

"Thank heavens! I thought you were going to give me the same treatment as mother. Em, you are a wretch. When can I see you?"

They spoke easily and naturally, as if they had known each other intimately for many years. There was no awkwardness or shyness arising from their last meeting. They could have been lovers, coming together again after the space of a day or two.

"Last time you saw me you ran off."

"I won't this time."

"What became of your chivalry?"

"I'm not sure. I only know that I have to see you, alone."

"Are you married?"

"Not yet. Are you?"

She gave him a steady look.

"No, I told you there would never be anyone but you and I meant it."

"It's different for me. No, damn it, that's just an excuse."

"No, it really is different for you and I understand that. Does your mother know who I am?"

"Heaven forfend, but she's suspicious of me."

"Why?"

"Because she knows I've been walking on air for the last few days."

"Why have you been doing that?" Her eyes held his; it was like an embrace. "Was it because you met Harry and he gave you my address? I had a note from him and he said he'd seen you."

"Yes, you abominable temptress, it was. Tonight, at about eleven?"

"Yes. I'll send the servants to bed. But, Nicholas."

"Mm?"

"Make quite certain that you want to come and, if you

do, don't walk away again.''

They were standing close together as they had done in the country lane near her cottage. He still filled her with wonder and a desire which was difficult to control. He half raised his hand; then he let it drop. Once he touched her, however briefly, he would take her in his arms and then the whole of London would know the truth.

"I won't, I promise. Madame Virot.''

"Yes?''

"I adore you.''

"Viscount Asterly.''

"Yes?''

"I love you. Don't be late.''

She turned away and left him and for a moment he took refuge in one of the window-seats, so that the girls shouldn't see what Em had done to him. She had been lovely before, but now she was more ravishing than the Venus de Milo.

For a second he paused to think about what he had done. He had burnt his boats and with them his conscience. When he visited Em at the appointed hour it wouldn't be to make polite conversation with her, or to enquire how she and his mother had got on with the latter's dresses.

When he saw Em that night he was going to take her to bed and his heart began to sing again as he leaned back and waited for Juliet to reappear.

Emerald sent the servants to bed. early. Mrs Grisdale, Maisie and Bert had elected to stay with the new owners of the Bloomsbury house. They had got used to the area and their friends were there, the thought of the Cort Street house overawed them.

Now Emerald had a butler, three maids, a cook, a coachman and a stable-lad, as well as Verity her personal maid and devoted companion. Verity had a cold and was confined to bed, so no explanations were necessary as far as she was concerned.

Quinney, the butler, was used to high-flyers like

Madame Virot, his face impassive when she told him the
staff could stop work at ten. He didn't need a nudge or a
wink to know what she was going to get up to. However, he
didn't presume to censure her; a woman with her looks was
bound to have a hundred and one admirers.

Nicholas arrived on the stroke of eleven, admitted by
Emerald herself. From the moment she opened the door the
sensual excitement began. They said nothing at first, for
silence had always suited them. She turned out the lights
and he followed her upstairs.

When they reached the bedroom she turned to face him,
more alive than she had ever been before. She kept very still
as he took a lock of her hair between his fingers, watching
the pleasure in him.

"Now you're a bit more like the girl I met seven years
ago, yet you really have changed."

"So have you." She didn't mind the preliminaries; it
would make the final union more perfect. "When you left
me in that wood you were so sad and you said it was over. I
wanted you more than the air I breathed, but you wouldn't
inflict what you called an injury. Do you remember? You
said you couldn't steal what would one day belong to
another man. When did you change your mind?"

"I remember. As to when I changed my mind, I'm not
sure. Perhaps from the very second I rode away, but it
wasn't until I met Harry Pentreath and he told me where
you lived that I knew even honour wasn't as important as
loving you." He touched her cheek as he had done before.
"Earlier today you were so grand and worldly. Now, in that
white wrap you're wearing, you look as pure and innocent
as you did when I first saw you."

She hoped he hadn't noticed the flash of fear in her eyes.
It wasn't only that she was cheating him; she was forced to
recall what it had been like when Noah had raped her. A
small part of that act would have to be repeated, or
Nicholas would know she wasn't a virgin, however much
she might look like one.

"Do I? But you said I'd altered."

"You know you have. You've become famous and you carry it off with a great air."

She gave a wry smile.

"Poor Emily Tregellan, fisherman's daughter, kitchenmaid and pot-scrubber. By the way, I call myself Emerald. I have done for years."

"Emerald to match your eyes? I shall call you Em, as Harry does. He loves you too, but I suppose you know that."

"Yes, and I'm fond of him."

"Then I'm sorry for him."

She gave a mock pout.

"Because I'm fond of him?"

"Because you don't love him."

She felt him stroke her neck, her lips parting as he bent to kiss them. He led her to the bed, their eyes still locked.

"Last time I undressed myself." Her voice was very low. "This time, if you want me, you're going to have to do it."

"I'm not very good with fastenings."

"After all the practice I'm sure you've had?"

They were just words, filling in a small piece of time. Their open mouths met again. Once, twice, three times; briefly, fleetingly, building up the tension of the moment. Then his fingers ran slowly down her back.

"No fastenings."

She shook her head, shivering as he drew the négligé from her shoulders and let it fall to the floor. His hands were feather-light on her body, skimming over the warm skin with a sure, erotic touch. When she moaned aloud he picked her up and threw her across the bed, still looking down at her as he removed his own clothes.

"Too late now, Em," he said and pulled her into his arms. "You had your chance to get away, but I'll never let you go now."

"I don't want to get away." His grip was brutal but it made her back arch in ecstasy, her lips searching for his again. "I never did want to escape."

The feel of him lying over her made her head reel and when he murmured her name again she cried out in desperation.

"Stop talking and make love to me. My darling, for God's sake make love to me or I shall die. Don't be gentle; not now. Hurt me ...hurt me ...oh, Nicholas, yes, yes, yes ...!"

Over the next week they met secretly. It wasn't easy, for the countess's surveillance was as diligent as ever. Nicholas made excuses, lied, not even batting an eyelid as he made his exodus and left Juliet more disturbed than ever. Selwyn's latest efforts to marry off his son was holding most of his attention; the niece of a marchioness this time. The countess thought she was an insipid wench, but she supported the earl enthusiastically. The sooner Nicholas was married the better. Whoever he was meeting was not of their own social circle, that was quite certain, and men in love did dangerous things.

One night Nicholas and Emerald sat together on a sofa, her head on his shoulder. They had made love as passionately and satisfyingly as on the first occasion. Now they were content to hold each other's hand without saying a word. In the end it was Nicholas who broke the silence.

"Em."

"Mm?"

"I want you to marry me."

Emerald caught her breath, feeling her happiness threatened.

"Dearest, that isn't possible. You've always said so. Your father would never agree."

"He won't know until it's all over."

"But one can't get married secretly. Of course he would know."

He looked down at her, his smile tender.

"We can elope to Gretna Green. We wouldn't be the first

to do so and we shan't be the last, now that Fleet Marriages are a thing of the past. Well, will you be my wife?"

She resisted, not wanting to face the agonising decision looming ahead of her.

"But is it legal?"

"Perfectly; I made quite sure of that. Why do you hesitate? Don't you love me enough to face the wrath of my parents?"

She laid her head against his chest so that he couldn't see her expression, her mind in turmoil. It was one thing to have become his mistress without telling him about Penrose, Feverell and the lost baby; quite another to become his wife. Her lips began to move silently, framing words which had no sound. Now was the time she had to make her confession; it couldn't be put off any longer. She accepted, as she had done once before, that if he knew the truth she would lose him. He would walk away again, but this time he would never come back. It wouldn't have been so hard if they had not become lovers, but now she knew the wonder of being part of Nicholas. His love kept her alive and if he left her she would fade away like a phantom at the dawning of a day.

"Em?"

He was demanding an answer, not understanding why she waited. She raised her head and smiled at him, casting the die.

"Yes, I'll marry you, if you're sure. Will your father ever forgive you?"

"Probably not, but I don't care. I shall have you."

When he had left her she went to her dressing-table and looked at her pallor. Nicholas hadn't noticed it; he'd been too full of plans for their flight. Even though she was about to go to bed, she touched her cheeks with rouge. She would probably have to do so many times in the future to hide her guilt and sorrow.

Then she took a handkerchief, rubbing the artificial colour away. She was being absurd. She had had her chance to be honest and she had let it pass. Now she would have to live the rest of her days with the lie lodged in her heart, but she would have Nicholas.

"Emily Tregellan," she said, addressing herself by a name she hadn't used for years. "Stop being a weak-kneed simpleton. You wanted him and now you've got him. What's done is done, so stop grizzling and decide what you want to pack. In two days you'll be in Gretna Green, your ladyship. How about that for a fisherman's daughter?"

Verity, still feeling poorly, hadn't the courage to ask if her mistress had told the viscount about her past, but Eugene Ryan was quite blunt. He was also alarmed. They had grown to be good friends and one night Emerald had told Eugene about Nicholas, but that was when she hadn't expected to see the latter again.

"I met Asterly once," said Ryan, and his usual smile was missing. "He's not like that boy Harry you've talked about. Nicholas Roman is a very different animal. He's charm itself on the surface but beneath that he's steel. I know all about men like him; met plenty of them in my time. If he should ever find out about you, he'll destroy you."

Emerald felt her flesh creep, for she knew Eugene was right. She also knew she should tell Nicholas the truth, but she couldn't.

"He won't find out," she replied, willing Nicholas to remain in ignorance. "Not unless you or Verity tell him."

"Neither of us will, but you're playing with fire."

"I know. It's like the moth and the candle, isn't it, but I can't help it. I love him too much."

"Then say your prayers, Em," said Ryan quietly, "because before you're finished you're going to need God's help. You should have stuck to Harry; you'd have been safe with him. In Viscount Asterly's hands I'm not so sure."

After the ceremony at Gretna Green Nicholas wrote to his father. It wasn't a pleasant task, but the earl couldn't be kept in the dark any longer. It was the viscount's hope that by the time he and Em had travelled leisurely back to London his parents would have got over the worst of their anger.

When his son's note reached him the earl had already returned to Cloverley Park. He read the letter, each word like a sword stabbing into his flesh.

"Selwyn? What is it?"

Juliet hurried to his side. For the first time she realised that he was getting older. Even though they had a grown son, she still thought of herself and her husband as they had been at their first meeting. Now she couldn't blind herself to the passing of the years any longer.

"My dear."

The earl spoke absently, as if he didn't really see her.

"Selwyn! Tell me what's wrong. Is it Nicholas? Has there been an accident?"

At last he looked up from the paper he was holding in a tight fist.

"No, it wasn't an accident. He did it deliberately."

"Did what? For heavens sake!"

"He got married. He says here that you know the woman; it seems you buy your clothes from her and know her as Madame Virot."

Juliet was the colour of chalk and she swayed on her feet.

"Oh, my dear, I'm sorry, I'm sorry." The earl was full of contrition as he helped her to a chair. "I shouldn't have broken the news so abruptly. Forgive me."

The countess forced herself to speak calmly, but Radfield could see what an effort it was.

"No, it is I who should beg your forgiveness. I knew there was something going on. I realised that Nicholas was seeing a woman, but I didn't know who she was. In my heart I felt it was different from his usual flirtations. I shouldn't have kept my anxieties to myself; I ought to have sought your advice. Then you could have stopped this madness."

"Don't blame yourself. If I hadn't been so busy trying to

arrange a betrothal with the Stewart girl, I would have seen it for myself."

"How could they have got married so quickly and without us finding out?"

"They went to Gretna Green."

"Oh no!"

"Sordid, I agree. Tell me, is she beautiful?"

The countess was on the point of denying it vehemently, not wanting to associate such a word with the cunning vixen who had robbed her of her son, but the words seemed to come out of her mouth before she could stop them.

"Yes, she is. I think perhaps she's the loveliest girl I've ever seen."

"She has bewitched him, damn her!"

Juliet laid her cheek against Radfield's hand and he could feel her tears.

"She snared him, like I snared you."

His fingers tightened over hers as he said quietly:

"It isn't quite the same thing. You were a baron's daughter; she is in trade. The blasted girl's a dressmaker."

Juliet sat up straight, her weakness over as she gave her husband a smile tinged with irony.

"No, you're quite right, you always are. It's a very different thing, as you say. I never did learn to sew properly. Well, my love, what do you suggest we do now?"

SEVEN

When they found the earl and countess had returned to Cornwall, Nicholas and Emerald made their way to Cloverley Park.

It was late when they finally drew up outside the front door, footmen hurrying forward to collect their luggage from the chaise. There were many surreptitious stares from the servants, but one particular footman drew back behind a pillar, his lips forming a soundless whistle.

Maids were summoned to escort Emerald to her room, for Nicholas had told her on the journey that he wished to see his parents alone before introducing her to his father.

Radfield was in the library, a glass of brandy in his hand. He gave his son a brief glance and then went back to his drink.

"You got my letter?" The viscount kept his tone cool. It wasn't going to be an easy interview, but at least his mother had gone to bed. "It reached you safely?"

"Of course."

"Father, I'm sorry it had to be this way, but I knew you'd never agree to the match."

"You were right." Radfield looked up again. "Christ Almighty, Asterly, do you realise what you've done?"

"I've married the woman I love."

"You've married a common seamstress."

Nicholas could feel his temper rising.

"Hardly that."

"Because she panders to rich women's fancies and plies

her needle in Belgravia? Don't be a fool. She's still a dressmaker. Why did you do this? You know what plans I had for you; how much I wanted you to have an heir."

"God willing I shall have one."

"By a workwoman."

"By my wife, my lord."

"Wife or not, your son will be tainted and not fit to bear our name."

"Damn it, you are being insufferably pompous."

"Don't speak to me like that. You aren't the injured party, I am. Don't you understand, even now, what you've done to me?"

The eyes of the two men met and Asterly felt his heart contract. It wasn't only anger he was reading in his father, but suffering too. For some reason he hadn't expected that. It was an unpleasant jolt and he said slowly:

"I'm sorry. What I did was not intended to wound you; you know I would never want that. I love Emerald."

"Emerald!"

"Her real name is Emily but I call her Em."

The earl was himself again, determined that his son would not catch him off guard again.

"Well don't expect me to do the same."

"But you will receive her?"

"I've no choice, have I? Go now, if you please. This conversation is finished."

After Nicholas had gone, Chatworth the butler, came quietly into the library.

"Not tonight, Chatworth, whatever it is. Leave it until to-morrow."

"I would, my lord, if it weren't for the importance of the matter. When Stubbs told me ..."

The earl frowned. Chatworth was very well trained. He would have left the room immediately he had been dismissed, unless what he had to say was of real urgency.

"Stubbs? Well, go on now you've started. What did Stubbs tell you?"

"That he knows the viscountess, my lord. Leastways, he saw her when she lived here in Cornwall."

The earl tried to maintain an emotionless front, but the niggle of fear was hard to put aside. He nodded, waving a careless hand.

"All right. You'd better explain."

Radfield listened in silence, his heart turning to stone.

"I'm sorry to be the one who had to bring this to you, my lord." The butler didn't like his master's colour. The earl's face was almost grey and the hand holding the glass wasn't quite steady. "Perhaps I shouldn't have said anything, but I can't be sure that Stubbs will keep quiet about it."

"You were quite right to put the facts before me." Radfield steeled himself against Chatworth's obvious concern. "We can't deal with this tonight, it's too late. I have no idea whether my son is aware of the truth or not. I shall find out in the morning. Meanwhile, ask Stubbs to oblige me by keeping a still tongue in his head. If he doesn't, he won't work for me any more and I'll see to it that no one else will employ him either. Not a word of this must get past these walls, is that understood?"

"Yes, my lord."

Chatworth bowed and finally the earl rose. He didn't want to have to tell Juliet, but he had no choice. He couldn't let her find out at the same time as questions were put to Asterly. He got to the door and then paused for a moment.

"Damn you, Nicholas," he said under his breath. "If you knew about this I hope your soul will rot in hell. If you were aware of what she was, I'll never forgive you as long as I live."

Nicholas and Emerald had been out for an early morning ride. Asterly wanted to clear the cobwebs away before he encountered his father again. He gave Emerald a quick smile as they entered the house.

"It won't be too bad. Be brave; they'll soon get used to

the idea."

He didn't really believe that but he had to keep her spirits up and when Chatworth informed him that the earl wanted to see him in the library he nodded, squeezing Emerald's hand to comfort her.

"Come along, sweetheart, let's get it over with. Keep you chin up."

Beneath the smart riding-habit Emerald's legs were shaking and when she saw the earl and countess standing by the fireplace she felt a sudden shudder go through her. There was something very wrong. She hadn't expected a welcome, but it was more than distaste for their son's choice of wife which made Nicholas's parents look as they did.

Asterly thought so too, and frowned.

"My lord, what is it?"

"You don't know? You really don't know?"

"If you are still talking about my marriage ..."

"I'm not, at least, not simply the ceremony which I hope to prove invalid in the course of time."

"It was legal, I can assure you." The viscount was bleak. "Well, if not that ...what?"

"Is it true that you knew this girl when she lived in Cornwall?"

Emerald couldn't swallow. It was as if someone had a hand round her throat. The earl had found out about her; she knew it. She could read it in his eyes, hear it in his voice.

"Yes, we met here."

"Did you know she was a prostitute?"

"How dare you, sir!"

"She's a trollop, Asterly. Are you telling me you didn't know that?"

"If she is, then I made her one. Yes, I slept with her before we were married."

"That's not what I'm talking about."

Nicholas's lips thinned.

"Then what are you talking about?"

"You remember Stubbs, I take it?"

"One of our footmen?"

"Yes. When he saw this wretched woman arrive he recognised her."

"Be good enough not to refer to the viscountess in such terms."

The earl bared his teeth.

"I'm still not sure whether you're a rogue or a fool. Listen to the story which Stubbs told Chatworth last night and which Chatworth in turn told me. Then tell me how to address this ...this creature. You see, Stubbs has a cousin, William Pettifer. He's a groom at Rowett Lodge, which is owned by Jehu Feverell. I'm sure you've heard of the unsavoury Mr Feverell."

Nicholas was very grim and Emerald felt as if she were afloat on a rough sea. The room wavered and circled about her, sickness coming over her in waves as she waited for the storm to break.

"Yes, I've met him. What of it?"

"You also know that your wife worked for him?"

"Yes."

The earl's eyes passed over Emerald and she felt unclean. He had made dirt of her with a single glance.

"One day Stubbs visited Pettifer at Rowett Lodge, where the latter had obtained a job not long before. He saw your paramour and commented on her appearance. Pettifer laughed and told him he stood no chance with her, for she was Feverell's mistress. It seems she also conceived a child by him, which she conveniently lost before anyone noticed that she was pregnant."

The viscount had lost some of his colour and his voice was uncertain.

"How could Pettifer have known that? Surely if it were common gossip Mrs Feverell would have been aware of it. This is simply unfounded scandal."

"Mrs Feverell was just about to go away when Pettifer took up his post. The liaison between her husband and this

woman started the moment her back was turned. As to the
baby, Pettifer overheard two maids discussing it some
weeks later. He gathered they had been present when the
miscarriage occurred and one said what a good thing it had
been that only two or three of the servants knew about the
matter. Then the other said that Mrs Feverell's personal
maid had seen Feverell going into your wife's room at night
while her mistress was absent. Both girls agreed Feverell
had to be the father; there was no one else it could have
been. But that's not all."

"It's enough!" Nicholas was violent. "I don't believe it."

"It's patently true. Why should those two maids have
discussed a fictitious situation? It was obvious that they
were sympathetic to your wife, according to Pettifer, and he
had no reason to lie either. But please allow me to continue,
for the rest is equally illuminating.

"Pettifer also told Stubbs that when he was younger he
had been to a harvest supper at Trefusis Farm. His father
was a cowherd there and the boy was allowed to attend
because it was his fourteenth birthday. It seems that after
the meal your wife, then fifteen years old, was found in a
cowshed with a man. She was stark naked and she had lain
with him. Her father found her and others crowded into the
shed too, among them Pettifer and his father. When he got
to Rowett Lodge and saw this woman again he said
nothing, realising she was a favourite of Mrs Feverell's and
later had become Feverell's doxy. He didn't want to get into
trouble and lose his job so he kept quiet, but he felt safe
enough confiding in his cousin.

"As I have said, there were dozens of witnesses to that
earlier incident; I could get you proof about your wife and
Feverell too, if you need it. When Pettifer saw her last night
and realised who she was, he felt it was his duty to tell
Chatworth. Well, why don't you ask her if I'm right?"

Nicholas's hand tightened on the riding-crop he was
carrying and for the first time he turned to look at Emerald.

She saw that he was now deadly white, his eyes filled with an emotion he had no idea how to handle. She knew her expression had betrayed her even before he began to frame his question. She had gambled and had lost.

She didn't let him put his demand into words; it would add insult to injury. It was over and that was that. She straightened her shoulders, glad that the room was stable again.

"Yes, it's true. It isn't as simple as it sounds, but I can't deny that those things happened."

"Nicholas!" Juliet broke the discipline of a lifetime as she cried out, her poise crumbling. "My dearest boy."

"Please be quiet, Mother." The viscount turned back to his father. "Sir, will you take my word that I had no knowledge of these matters? I married without your consent or blessing, but I would never have done this to you knowingly."

The earl saw the terrible look on his son's face. The bottom had dropped out of Asterly's world and he had become a changed man in a matter of a few minutes.

"Yes, I believe you. I didn't think you knew, but I had to be absolutely certain. What are you going to do?"

"With your permission I would like to speak to my wife alone."

"Certainly, but take her to the Dower House. This is my home and I don't want it further polluted."

Nicholas's fingers were like pincers as they dug into Emerald's arm. The first blank disbelief in Nicholas was passing and with it his control. She saw the raw fury in him and was petrified, but Radfield hadn't finished yet.

"Asterly."

"My lord?"

"Don't bring her back. I don't want her under my roof again."

"I shan't, have no fear of that. Mother, I ask forgiveness for inflicting this on you; it was quite unpardonable. Now, madam." The hand tightened a further degree. "Come with me, if you please. We have some unfinished business to attend to."

The Dower House was seldom used. There were covers over the furniture, shutters across every window but one. That hung on a broken hinge, letting in some light.

As Asterly pushed Emerald into the main sitting-room he felt as if he were on his deathbed. Life was oozing from every pore, sapping his spirit and his strength. Lethal anger lapped over shock, his mind unable fully to assimilate what had happened. If Em had denied his father's charges, he would have taken her side, but she hadn't. The thought of her in another man's bed made him want to vomit, but at least it finally brought reality and acceptance rushing out of chaos.

The only part of him which was untouched was his heart. Whatever Em had done, he still loved her as much as ever and he knew he always would. The weakness in him increased his fury and he was half mad as he spun her round.

"Well?"

His voice was the cut of a knife and she flinched.

"I told you it wasn't as simple as it sounded."

"It seems plain enough to me. You used men before when it suited you. Now you've used me."

"No, that isn't true! I adore you."

"Liar! If you had even a semblance of affection for me, you'd have told me about yourself."

"I tried to ...I wanted to ...so much, but I couldn't bring myself to do it. I knew you'd never understand and that I'd lose you."

He hardly heard her. Pain was gnawing at him as he let flow a stream of invective which scalded her, eating down to her bones.

"Do you really expect me to believe that?" he asked when his curses had stopped. "You wore a mask; sweet

purity on the surface, evil rotting away beneath it. You
didn't care a damn about me, did you? I was just another
buffoon for you to manipulate. You wanted to dangle me on
a string as you did the others.''

"No! It was you who came to my house that night. You
who wanted to make love to me. I didn't persuade you.''

"You bloody whore!''

He struck her across the face with the back of his hand,
watching her fall.

"You didn't stop me, did you?'' He stood over her, the
lines round his mouth making Emerald catch her breath.
"You didn't tell me I was just one of many. You even went
through the farce of making me think you were a virgin.''

"Yes, I did.'' She propped herself up on one elbow, half
stunned by his blow. "But it was because I loved
you ...needed you, Nicholas. It wasn't the way you think.''

"And when I asked you to marry me.'' He ignored her
protest. "You were play-acting again, trying to convince me
that you were worried about my father and what he would
say. You were out to get me, weren't you, just as you got
your first man when you were fifteen. You disgust me.''

Suddenly Emerald hit back, for she had nothing to lose.
She wouldn't see Nicholas after this and his tirade of scorn
and loathing forced her into retaliation.

"To hell with you, my lord! Her eyes glittered with her
own rage. "How dare you make yourself judge and jury
without giving me a hearing? A servant goes running to the
earl with gossip and you lap it all up. You haven't asked to
hear my side of things.''

"I don't want to. You admitted what you'd done.''

"I said those things had happened; now I'm going to tell
you why and how.''

"I'm not interested. Do you think I want to hear the
sordid details of your *affaires*, starting with the poor
blockhead you entrapped at that harvest supper?''

He was a totally different person from the one she had
held in her arms: not the same man she had married at

Gretna Green. She could feel resentment as bitter as gall flood through her because he wouldn't give her a chance.

"Listen to me, damn you! I didn't trap anyone. That night a man called Penrose came up behind me and put his hand over my mouth so I couldn't scream for help. Then he dragged me into a cowshed. He tore my clothes off, pawed me with his dirty hands, and then he raped me. No one believed me innocent; they were all like you. Of course it had to be my fault. I was a woman; a scarlet woman. My father turned me out of the house. That's when I went to work for Feverell. Nothing happened until his wife went away."

Asterly's eyes were blank and disbelieving.

"And then I suppose he dragged you into your bedroom after gagging you."

"No, he didn't." She took a deep breath, knowing she was losing the fight. Eventually, she might have been able to get Nicholas to believe her version of the encounter with Noah, but she had thrown away her only grain of hope because she had said yes to Jehu. "He came to my room. I knew that if I refused him he'd send me away. He wouldn't have allowed me anywhere near Whitewater, so I shouldn't have been able to go on learning with Miss Pezzach. Most of all, if I went right away I'd never have the chance of seeing you. And I did want to see you; you'll never know how much. I had to make a quick decision. I'd already lost my virtue, as they say; I had to keep on dressmaking; I had to be near you. Since I never expected even to speak to you, I thought the only thing for me was to save all I could and get to London. I needed money to open a shop and although Feverell didn't pay much, it helped. That's why I let him stay; for those reasons."

Nicholas wasn't listening to her. He was picturing her with Feverell. He'd seen the man and that made the images worse. Emerald naked in the merchant's arms; the man's plaything. Feverell gloating over her, slobbering as he took her.

"You cheap slut." He wouldn't heed his heart, for that was betraying him as surely as Emerald had done. That still kept hammering home the fact that he worshipped her. He tried to silence it by the voice of reason as he cursed her again. "I feel degraded because I've touched you; defiled because I made our bodies one."

"You stupid fool," she shouted, her frustration exploding all over him. "You and your precious feelings. You said you loved me. If that had been true you'd still do so, no matter what I'd done. I wouldn't care what sins you'd committed in the past: I'd go on loving you just the same. You don't know what true love means, nor what life is all about. You think I'm scum because I did what I did for money. Money doesn't mean anything to you because you've always had plenty.

"You haven't gone to bed on bare boards, crying yourself to sleep because you were starving. You didn't get cut feet from walking on stone and pebbles without shoes. You didn't have to clear up children's sick, scrub floors, work nearly twelve hours a day and then go home and rake out the pig's sty, mend nets, do the washing and watch your sister coughing up blood.

"Yes, I made Feverell pay because at that time I thought only money could give me any kind of existence, but after that day in the wood, no man has ever touched me nor ever will."

"Others are poor; as poor as you were." He spat the words at her. "Not all of them sell themselves and I doubt if many could have lied and cheated as expertly as you did in order to get me. Oh, yes, you were very good; very good indeed. You even managed to satisfy me in bed to get what you wanted, although pleasing men in that way must have been very tedious for you. After all, one man's needs are much like another's, aren't they?"

His voice dropped to a dreadful whisper and Emerald's teeth began to chatter. She hadn't got through to him at all; he hadn't wanted to understand anything she'd said and now he looked like a man bent on murder.

"You will leave here at once," he said, "and you will never come back. I don't want to see you – ever again. You've made a fool of me and you've ruined my life, for now I can never have the heir my father wanted so much. I shall have to spend all my years knowing you're my wife and I hope that God grants me an early death."

She made one last appeal in spite of her fear, knowing it would be useless.

"Whatever you think of me now, and however much you despise me, I really do love you. When we were in bed it wasn't pretence on my part. I wanted you ...you are everything to me." She could hardly get the words out because his look was smothering them with dread. "I ...I ...will always remember you."

His smile was dreadful and she tried to crawl away from him. Like lightning, one riding-boot came down on her ankle, making escape impossible.

"Yes, you'll remember me, but not for my loving," he said and brought his whip down hard across her back. "You've got a debt to pay, madam, and this is what you'll recall if, in the future, I should ever cross your mind. This, and this, and this and this, you ...she-devil! You may not bear my son, but by God you'll carry my bruises for a very long time to come.

Ryan was shocked by Emerald's appearance when he went to see her at Court Street.

"You can say 'I told you so' if you like," she said, trying to make a joke of it, her eyes blurred with tears. "I shan't mind."

"He found out?"

"His father did." She explained briefly, not blaming Stubbs. He had merely been loyal to his master. "The earl looked at me and I wanted to crawl under a stone."

"My dear."

"Don't be sorry for me, Eugene, or I shall give way completely."

"What about the business? Will you be able to go on working, or will the countess spread the word?"

Emerald shook her head.

"No, she won't do that. Nothing will ever leak out of Cloverley Park. Radfield will see to that. No, I shall go on as before."

"And Asterly?"

He saw her tremble.

"Don't think about it if you don't want to, Em. I shouldn't have asked."

"He thrashed me." She was talking to herself, remembering. "I didn't mind that so much because I deserved it. It was the hate ...the terrible, terrible hate. He cursed me in words I'd never heard before. His eyes looked as if ..."

"Yes?"

"As if he were half crazed. Then he sent me away and told me he'd never see me again. Oh, Eugene, how am I going to exist without him? I love him; I love him so very much."

Ryan took her in his arms, holding her close, saying nothing. There was nothing to say. When she drew away from him, he handed her a handkerchief and she managed a smile at last.

"You're a good friend. I'm glad you were here; you and Verity. It would have been awful to come home to nothing."

Verity was trying to keep composed for her mistress's sake, but her eyes were red when she joined Emerald later.

"Don't you start," said Emerald, forcing her voice to be steady. "One of us is bad enough."

"I'm so sad for you."

"Don't be. I don't want sympathy, I need help. I've got to get on with things. Become more famous; make more money. It's all that's left for me now. When you first came to work for me, you were stern enough; you've got to be the same again."

"I'll try."

"Good girl." For a moment the two women's hands touched. Then Emerald said briskly: "Now what about some tea? Nothing like a good cup of tea to get one moving. I'll swallow my sorrows with a lump of sugar, as my ma used to say. Better get me two lumps today, Verity; I've got a lot of sorrow to get down my neck."

The day after Emerald's departure the earl listened to his son's suggestion, concerned by the viscount's appearance.

"You don't have to move to the Dower House. There's no reason why you shouldn't stay here. It's your home."

Asterly's fury was spent; he reminded the earl of a sleepwalker.

"Thank you, Father, but I think it would be for the best. You and Mother need time to heal. So do I."

"As you wish. I'll give orders for the place to be made ready for you."

It occurred to Nicholas in passing that his father's manner had changed completely. There was no longer any heat or ire in him. Probably it was because Em had gone, although the ramifications of the marriage couldn't have escaped his father. On religious and other grounds, the earl would never countenance divorce. He shrugged it off as imagination and said:

"I'll probably buy a house in London. I shall go abroad now and then too. I don't want to be pinned down in any one place. I have to be free."

"I understand."

"Do you, sir?"

Radfield gave a slight smile.

"Why is it children always imagine their parents are hatched from an egg, fully matured and often with one foot in the grave? You forget; I was your age once."

"But nothing like this happened to you."

"No, it didn't. Nicholas, sit down and listen to me for a moment. When I first received your letter I was totally outraged. I had spent so much time planning your future. You would marry the bluest blood in England; my grandchildren would wear coronets. When I heard from Chatworth what manner of woman your wife was, my fury grew to such towering proportions that I could no longer control it. I bitterly regret the things I said to you the night you arrived and the morning after."

"You had every right to vent your spleen on me and that ...my wife."

"No, I didn't."

The viscount looked up. He had been right after all; his father was quite different.

"You have had a change of heart, my lord? I can scarcely believe that."

"I can appreciate your scepticism." Radfield was dry. "It was strange, now I come to think of it."

"What was?"

"The rapidity with which I saw it wasn't for me to choose the woman with whom you wished to spend your life. The way in which rage gave way to understanding in a single second."

Nicholas was frowning.

"I'm afraid I don't follow you."

"No, how could you, but it was really very simple. Last night I went to my bedroom, still full of anger and a kind of despair. Your mother was sitting at the dressing-table, brushing her hair. She looked to me just as she had done on the day I married her. In that one moment I knew beyond doubt that if someone told me she was a harlot I wouldn't have given a damn. I love her."

"You couldn't love her in such circumstances."

"Oh, yes I could; I would. It was then I realised it was the same for you. You love your wife; discovering the truth about her hasn't altered that."

"Of course it has. As far as I'm concerned she no longer exists."

The earl was compassionate.

"My dear boy, fool me by all means if you think you can. Don't fool yourself; it's too costly."

"I've told you; she means nothing to me now. Don't read in me things which aren't there."

"But they are there and I can see them. They were there yesterday morning; but I was too furious at the time to pay heed to them. It was only later, as I say, that my eyes were opened."

"I shan't bring her back here."

"That is up to you."

"I'll never see her again."

"Possibly not, but you know what I'm saying is true. You won't stop caring for her. Yours is as much a love-match as mine was, and morals and breeding have no part to play in such things."

The viscount held out a moment or two longer; then he gave in.

"No, you're right. They say life plays tricks on one, don't they and it's played the cruellest jest of all on me. I'm in love with a prostitute and there's nothing I can do about it. Forgive me, Father, I must go."

Asterly went into the Dower House, to the room with the broken shutter. He could see Emerald lying on the floor, the mark of his hand on her cheek. He clenched his teeth and opened the other shutters, hoping she wasn't going to haunt the place. Then he sat down on a chair, wishing he could feel good, healthy anger again. He couldn't because there was none left. There was just an overwhelming sense of loss and a heart which ached so much he could have cried out in torment.

He was sorry for the hurt he'd caused his parents; his father had so wanted their House to continue. He had been surprised at the earl's perception and the way he had spoken of love. He'd always been aware of the fondness his mother and father had for each other, but somehow had never thought of them sharing the sort of passion he and Emerald had known. The earl had been right about that, too. Children never saw their parents as warm, red-blooded human beings. To imagine them in bed together made for a sort of embarrassment.

He went out into the sunlight, shielding his eyes. He was twenty-three years old and the world had come to an end for him.

"Dear heaven," he said aloud, not caring if anyone heard him or not. "I wish I were dead. Oh, Em, my darling, I wish to God I were dead.

EIGHT

"Of course I'm certain." Emerald gave Eugene a mildly exasperated look. "You sound just like Jehu Feverell did. I was sure then, and I'm sure now. I'm going to have Nicholas's baby."

"Then you must tell him so."

"No." She was sharp and very definite. "He's not to know about this; not ever."

Ryan was equally short.

"Em, that's absurd. You must tell him. It isn't fair to him. It's as much his as yours."

"He should have thought about that before he turned me out."

"He didn't know you were pregnant then."

Emerald gave her partner a sardonic smile.

"He might have considered the possibility. Such things do happen when a man and a woman make love."

"You're being unreasonable."

"So was he, and cruel too. No, Eugene, he's not to be told. Give me your word you'll say nothing to him. Promise me!"

Ryan gave way. It wasn't his business and he left Emerald ringing the bell for Verity to give her her instructions.

"I want the whole staff to go."

"All the servants, madam?" Verity was taken aback. "But why?"

"Because I'm not sure whether any of them ever saw my husband come to this house. I don't want another Stubbs.

Give them each a year's wages and write out good
references for them and I'll sign them. Then get new people
in. I'm a widow; my husband died in a hunting accident. Is
that clear?"

"Yes, of course, if that's how you want it to be."

"It's how it's got to be." Emerald's hardness melted and
she gave Verity an apologetic look. "Sorry, I didn't mean to
bite your head off. I'm nervous, I suppose."

"You don't think ..."

"No, I don't. I've just told Eugene that the viscount is
never to know. I say the same thing to you."

"Very well."

"Verity."

"Yes, madam?"

"If it's a girl, we can teach her to sew, can't we? But if it's
a boy ..." She had to screw up every ounce of self-control to
go on. "If it's a boy it might be like Nicholas. Then I shall
never have a chance to forget him."

Verity, who had been on her way to the door, turned back,
her eyes sad.

"You won't forget him anyway, child or no child. The
kind of love you have for Viscount Asterly is incurable."

"I know." Emerald's voice was very low, filled with tears.
"Do you think I don't realise that? I worship the ground he
walks on, but I wish I'd never met him. Oh God! Why did I
ever have to meet him? I love him, but I'm never going to
see him again. I'd be better off in my grave, wouldn't I?"

Emerald's son, Robert, was born in 1843 and two years
later she decided to visit Paris. The boy, so like his father
that she almost wept every time she looked at him, was
healthy, endearing and so well behaved that she had no
qualms about leaving him in Verity's charge, with a nanny
to help her. The new staff was efficient and had never
doubted the story of their mistress's widowhood.
Everything would run smoothly, with Eugene keeping an
eye on the business.

Ryan had given Emerald letters of introduction to two of the foremost dressmakers in Paris, Madame Delatour and Madame Palmyre. He had also arranged for a Madame Virginie Feuillet to act as his partner's companion and chaperon. She was English-born, so language would be no problem, and she knew all the places which would be of interest to Emerald.

It was early summer when Emerald disembarked at Boulogne and the hour was late. She had enjoyed the journey from the moment the cross-Channel steamer had left London Bridge, too excited to eat the excellent meals provided on board. She was determined to make another effort to put the past behind her. She was in France, on her way to see the city which was the heart and beating pulse of fashion.

Early next morning she drank coffee at a small table outside a café while she and her fellow passengers waited for the coach which was to take them to the capital.

When at last the vehicle rumbled into Paris, Emerald was enchanted by her first sight of the city. One of the postilions was English and she cried out in delight to him.

"Oh, isn't it beautiful? It's so pale and clean after London. The sky is pure azure and even the gutters look like silver."

"Water-carts 'ave just been by, ma'm," said the man, who was used to the capital and hardened to its charms. "Not all of it is as good as this. You want to keep out of the side-streets at night. They're dangerous and they stink."

"What are those places with pink glass in the windows and vines and golden railings? And the other shops with pieces of bright red, blue and yellow cloth flying outside?"

"First ones are wine shops; others haberdashers. "'Scuse me, ma'm. I've got to get the boxes down."

Madame Virginie Feuillet proved to be a brisk, energetic woman of about forty, who took Emerald under her wing like a mother hen. She was very thin, but most elegant and, as Eugene had said, knew her way around the city. They paid their respects to Mesdames Delatour and Palmyre at their respective *ateliers de couture*. The latter were much like their English equivalent, the same overworked girls, shoulders bent, eyes strained as they stitched away at gown after gown.

They went to Gagelin and Opigez, an extremely fashionable shop in the rue de Richelieu, where Emerald bought several lengths of material, going on to *La Maison de Caravane* for Indian foulards and Eastern silks. She picked up copies of the latest fashion magazines, *Le Follet*, *Le Petit Courrier des Dames* and *La Psyché* before turning her attention to Verdier, who as the master of canes and sunshades. Emerald hadn't lost her penchant for parasols and she was torn by indecision as she looked at those spread out before her. Handles of jade, ivory and gold; covers of silk and lace, some with feathers, some embroidered. She was still debating which to have, knowing she would purchase at least three, when a man standing next to her said sympathetically:

"It is so difficult, isn't it? If I were a woman I'd buy the lot, for I wouldn't be able to leave a single one behind."

Emerald found her hand being kissed, and then smiled at by a very handsome man with dark hair and eyes, impeccably dressed, who pronounced himself to be the Comte de Grancey.

Emerald wondered if Virginie would cluck with disapproval but she was simpering with pleasure instead. It seemed that to be acknowledged by Marcel Giradin, Comte de Grancey, was tantamount to royal patronage.

Emerald wasn't sure how it all began. The comte bought a dozen of the sunshades for her, brushing aside her objections. Then he swept her away, Virginie in tow, to the smartest restaurant in Paris.

After that came dinners, and late suppers when they left the theatres, and somehow Virginie was no longer there. When she told Marcel she had come to do some shopping, he insisted on accompanying her. He never allowed her to pay for a thing, even though she told him such generosity made her feel most uncomfortable.

"I have plenty of money to pay for the goods myself," she told him once, and quite severely. "There is no need for you to ...."

"There is every need," he had replied with a look which had made her colour up. "I am indulging myself and you will not stop me."

Then there were pearls, emeralds, rubies and diamonds. She tried to refuse them, but it was like assaulting an impregnable fortress. She knew what was coming and thought about it as she put the finishing touches to her toilet one night.

Men like the comte were not philanthropists. They were extremely generous when they wanted a woman, but the woman had to pay a price as well.

She had told Nicholas there would never be another man, but that had been a long time ago. She was young, with normal appetites, and she was lonely. Madame Feuillet's ability to fill the vacuum in her life was limited.

She considered herself in the long glass. She accepted that she was good to look at. Not only had she no false modesty, but many men, particularly Asterly, had said so. She knew she could please Marcel and it wouldn't mean a thing. He didn't love her, nor she him. It would have no more significance than enjoying a concert together.

When she joined the comte, she sensed it was the night he was going to invite her to his home. He would take her there at a late hour, and all the servants would have retired discreetly. She had one last spasm of doubt, and then gave in. If it didn't matter to Nicholas, it didn't matter to her, and the viscount wouldn't give a damn.

Marcel Giradin was faintly surprised when Emerald agreed to his proposition without demur. He had thought she would put on a show of reluctance, making him chase her. She didn't look like an ordinary strumpet, but one could never be certain of such things nowadays. He didn't really mind one way or the other. He simply wanted to get her between his sheets.

When he returned to his bedroom he found she hadn't started to undress. He frowned, put out because she seemed to be cheating him.

"*Chérie*? Is something wrong? Ah, perhaps it is all those fastenings which keep your delectable body from my hungry eyes."

He saw the violent shiver which went through her at his words, not understanding it. He didn't think she found him repulsive, yet he knew then that he would never possess her.

He sat on the edge of the bed, wondering why he wasn't angry. He had spent time and money and to no avail, but there was such agony in the girl that he couldn't ignore it.

"Come and sit beside me," he said gently. "I won't touch you; you have my word. Tell me about it; perhaps it will help."

She obeyed, her head bowed.

"Nothing will help."

"Is it that bad?"

"Yes."

"Who is he?"

Their eyes met and he saw fresh pain in hers.

"I can't tell you that. I can only say that I love him so much that I will never be able to sleep with you or anyone else. I'm sorry, Marcel; so very sorry. I didn't intend to behave like this. I thought I would be able to forget him for a while. Of course, I'll return all your gifts first thing tomorrow."

"There's no need for that."

"Of course there is." She was tart. "I couldn't possibly keep them in the circumstances."

"I want you to. Listen, my dear. Once in every man's lifetime there comes a woman who is different. He doesn't always know what makes her unlike the rest; he just knows she is. It's not the prospect of sexual satisfaction which makes him want to be with her. It's something else, but I can't explain it because I don't know the answer myself. For me, you were that woman. I won't see you again after tonight, but I'll never forget you. I might have given you a few pieces of coloured stone, but you've showered gifts on me which are beyond price. Your smile, your loveliness, your laughter and the grace with which you move. Those, and so much more. Keep my humble offerings, I beg you. They will be something for you to remember me by.''

For a second Emerald was back in the half-lit room in the Dower House at Cloverley Park. Nicholas had given her something to remember him by, but it hadn't been jewels, furs, fans and other fripperies. Yet she would never forget him for a single moment of a single day. In a week's time she would have forgotten that Marcel Giradin existed.

"Please?"

She nodded, pushing Nicholas away.

"I don't know how to thank you and not for the things you have bought me. You understand what I mean?"

"Of course. He's a lucky man, whoever he is."

A tear began to trickle down Emerald's cheek and she didn't hear the comte's exclamation of dismay.

"Lucky? Oh no, Marcel, he wasn't lucky. He was the most unfortunate man who was ever born and it was I who brought down the scourge upon him."

He let her cry, holding her as a father might hold his grieving child; then he took her back to her hotel.

"Do you know what was left in Pandora's box when everything else had gone?"

Emerald shook her head, feeling the strength of his hand on hers.

"No. What was left?"

"Hope. It is that which makes it possible for human beings to go on living. Never forget that, my dear. I gave you a jewel casket made of gold and silver. Don't put your necklaces and rings in it. Put hope in it instead. Look at it now and then, for whilst it remains in your possession not all is lost.''

"Dear Marcel. Do you have a box with hope in it, too?"

Momentarily a shadow passed over his face.

"I did have one, but I left the lid open and it flew away."

"I'm sorry. That was my fault."

He gave her a light kiss and then vanished into the darkness and Emerald went up to her room and stared at herself in the glass again. After a long while she said sadly:

"I said I wouldn't, Nicholas my dearest, and I won't. Next time I feel as I did this evening I'll open my casket instead. Oh, my love, my love, I wish I knew where you were. How I wish I could see you just once more."

Nicholas Roman had bought a house in London, but he seldom stayed in it. For nearly three years he travelled, returning to England occasionally to see his parents, restless to be off again.

He had just got back from Austria, breaking his journey in town. The comfortable residence in Grosvenor Street was kept in perfect order by the servants whether their master was there or not, but to Asterly it seemed to echo with emptiness.

When he went out for a walk he had no intention of going anywhere near Court Street. He didn't know whether it was sheer coincidence that he found himself turning into it, or whether some sourcery had led him there.

He didn't know why he rang the bell of Emerald's house either. He had sworn that he never wanted to see her again, yet there he was on the step, having no idea what he was going to say when the door opened.

A footman appeared, very courteous, for he recognised quality when he saw it, but once inside the viscount was even more at a loss for words. However, he had to say something. He wasn't sure whether Emerald's servants used her business name, but he was quite certain she wouldn't be using his, so he compromised.

"I would like to see your mistress, if you please."

"I'm sorry, sir, but Mrs Tregellan isn't here. She's in

Paris at the moment."

In a way it was a relief, or it should have been. Nicholas couldn't understand the rush of disappointment which filled him. He felt deflated, but was prepared to go on his way when he saw a nursemaid coming down the stairs holding a small boy by the hand.

Asterly's heart started to thud enevenly. One of his earliest memories had been peering into his mother's looking-glass, chuckling at his reflection. Looking at the boy was like seeing the mirror-image again.

By now, the butler had appeared and a parlourmaid in a crisp white apron and cap. They, and the footman, looked at Asterly and then back at the boy, something rippling among them like the wind in the treetops.

"Who is in charge of this child?" asked the viscount finally. "I want to see the person responsible for him while his mother is in France."

"Ah, that's Miss Dean, sir." The butler stepped forward to take charge of the extraordinary affair. Widow or not, there was no doubt who was Master Robert's father. "She's out shopping; won't be back for a while. May I enquire who is asking?"

"My name is Asterly; Viscount Asterly. This is my son and since his mother has chosen to go to Europe and leave him with servants, I'm taking him with me."

There was a renewed whisper, this time a nervous one. A man of importance and looking as fierce as Old Nick, yet the butler tried valiantly to withstand his unexpected visitor's demand.

"Well, my lord, I don't know that I can exactly let you do that. You see ..."

"You can't stop me," returned Nicholas curtly. "You are his nurse?"

The girl was shaken and pale with fright, but she nodded.

"Pack his things. You have ten minutes."

"My lord, you can't take him from his home like this."

"I'm taking him to his real home and you may inform your mistress, should she ever deign to come back from Paris, that I've returned to Cornwall. Will you go and get on with that packing, or do I have to make you?"

The nurse fled and Asterly went forward to look down at his son. The wide, innocent eyes met his own, inquisitive but not fearful, and when Nicholas picked him up, one small hand went out to touch his cheek. For a second he thought he was going to break down in front of Emerald's staff, but he managed to keep his face impassive. He had a son and she hadn't let him know. She had borne him an heir and hidden the fact from him.

It hurt almost as much as learning about Em's past and he was grateful when the nursemaid came rushing down the stairs again, boxes in hand, so that he was able to go.

"I don't know what Miss Dean will say." The butler realised he couldn't restrain the viscount; he also knew there was no shred of doubt about Master Robert's relationship with the tall, handsome man whose eyes were black with fury. "What shall I say?"

"What you like. Tell her the same as you're going to tell your mistress, and now get out of my way."

"But his mother ..."

"... has no idea how to care for him, otherwise she'd be here. Damn you! Will you open that door!"

Once back in his own house the viscount was faced with the fact that he needed help to get Robert to Cornwall. He had told Em's servants that she had no idea how to look after the child, but then neither had he. He looked helplessly at his progeny, weak as a kitten when Robert smiled at him, and heartily thankful when his own butler ventured to suggest that one of the maids, who had helped to bring up eight brothers and sisters, should accompany him on his journey.

He took the road to Cornwall in easy stages, for he didn't want Robert to get overtired, but eventually he reached

Cloverley Park and was met by Chatworth's look of incredulity.

"Shall I announce you, my lord?" asked the butler when he had recovered himself. "The earl is in the library."

"No, thanks, Chatworth; we'll surprise him, eh Robert?"

Radfield was working at his desk, writing a letter. He looked up and for a moment the pen shook in his hand. Then he laid it down and stood up.

"Father, this is Robert. He is ..."

Nicholas broke off, for it was obvious that the earl wasn't paying attention to him. Selwyn was staring down into the puzzled blue eyes, seeing the pink mouth quiver between a tentative smile and a droop to herald tears. It turned the clock back twenty odd years, for it was Nicholas as he had been at the same age. The shock had passed, but the earl was filled with another emotion a hundred times stronger.

"I know who he is," he said and smiled. "It is my grandson. Robert." He held out both his hands, waiting until the child had placed his own in them. "You are very welcome. Tell me; do you think you are too old to give me a kiss?"

It had been the viscount's intention that Robert should live in the Dower House with him, but his father brushed the idea aside at once.

"You go and stay there if you want to," he said, keeping the child close to his side, "but your mother wouldn't give me a minute's peace if I let you take him too. Come along, Robert. Let's go and find your grandmother, shall we?"

The next morning the earl was kneeling by his grandson's side, shewing him how to spin a top. Asterly watched them for a while, then he said hesitantly:

"Is he tainted? Do you think he's unfit to bear our name?"

The earl glanced up briefly.

"Don't be an idiot, Asterly. He's every inch a Roman. Go and find something useful to do. Robert and I are busy."

But later that day the earl was serious as he said quietly:

"What's going to happen when your wife returns?"

"I don't know, nor do I particularly care."

"She'll want the boy back."

"She won't get him. He's my son."

"And hers."

"She went away and left him."

"In good hands, I'm sure."

"He stays here."

Radfield sighed. Nicholas still wasn't ready to face up to facts; perhaps he never would be. Meanwhile, he intended to make the most of his grandson.

Asterly walked back to the Dower House with loneliness as his only companion. He went into the room where he and Emerald had last been together, feeling the very walls reproach him. Then he let indignation stiffen his sinews again.

She'd gone to Paris and left the boy; she hadn't even let him know about the child who had crept so quickly into his heart. If she was upset when she found that Robert had gone, she had no one to thank for it but herself.

He poured himself a drink and swallowed it in one gulp, trying not to care that he had missed the sight of his newly born son cradled against Em's breast. Then he went to the window and looked out on the well-trimmed hedges and lawns.

"Em," he said softly, "why didn't you let me know? Oh damn you, you heartless bitch! Why didn't you tell me?"

When Verity Dean returned from her shopping expedition and heard what had happened, she almost fainted. After the maids had given her a cup of strong tea, she ordered the carriage to be brought to the door and set off to see Eugene Ryan.

"Oh, my God," said Ryan. "How did he find out?"

"He just called at the house. The servants don't seem to know why. They say he didn't mention Robert; just asked for her ladyship. Then the nursemaid came down the stairs with the child and he saw him. The staff said they were like two peas in a pod; the viscount and Robert, I mean. They couldn't argue with him, for it was clear that he was the child's father. Mr Ryan, what on earth shall I do?"

"Go home, Verity, and stop worrying. I'll write to Em immediately and she'll be in London before you know it. Meanwhile, the boy's safe enough. He hasn't been abducted by a stranger."

"But how will Miss Emerald get him back? The servants who were present said the viscount looked furious because she wasn't there to look after him."

"It couldn't have been easy for him, confronted by a son he didn't know existed. I told Em she was wrong not to let him know. Even though they'd parted, he had a right to be informed."

"He'll try and keep Master Robert, won't he?"

Eugene looked grim. He was certain the viscount would do exactly that, and there was no point in keeping the truth from Verity.

"Yes, probably and he holds strong cards. Now, don't go blaming yourself for this. It was none of your doing."

"But if I'd been there ..."

Ryan gave a tight smile.

"Roman would still have taken him. I told Em once that underneath his charm that man was made of steel, but she wouldn't heed me. Now she knows I'm right. I've got a feeling that Viscount Asterly is going to be a nasty enemy. Getting Robert out of his hands will be the hardest fight Em has ever had to put up. God help her; I hope she's strong enough for what she's got to do."

NINE

As soon as Eugene Ryan's letter reached her, Emerald left Paris. She had felt sick and shaken when she had first read its contents; the anger came later.

Robert was more than a precious child to her. He was her only remaining link with Nicholas. He was Asterly's son and looking at him was like looking at the viscount himself.

She realised from the moment she got the news that getting Robert back wouldn't be easy. Asterly was bitter and vindictive, only too ready to inflict injury on her. She had had many blows in her life, but none as severe as the loss of her baby.

She wondered why Nicholas had gone to Court Street that day. He had said he never wanted to see her again and he couldn't have known about Robert. She had taken such precautions to ensure that the viscount wouldn't find out about him, but it had all been in vain. For whatever reason he had gone to the house he had found the perfect way of paying her back.

She knew she would have to go to Cornwall, once she had spoken to Verity and Eugene. That would mean seeing Nicholas again and as the carriage came to a stop outside her front door, she found the palms of her hands were damp. Although he would still loathe her, the mere prospect of looking into the deep blue eyes, being close to him, talking to him and remembering what had once been between them made her heart race. Her promiscuity had separated them for good, but it hadn't stopped what she felt for him. He had been the perfect lover and in his arms she had touched the fringe of heaven. Even after what he had just done, her need for him was as great as ever. Hers was a passion which wouldn't die until she did.

"I don't know what to say." Verity was in tears again. "I was out, you see, so ..."

"It's all right." Emerald was quite calm. "It wasn't your fault."

"But if I'd been here ..."

"You wouldn't have been able to stop him."

"That's just what Mr Ryan said."

"He was right. Pack some fresh things for me, will you? I shall start out for Cornwall later today. Meanwhile, I'm going up to Robert's room for a bit. See that I'm not disturbed."

Emerald looked at the empty bed, seeing in her mind's eye the smile Robert always gave her when she went to kiss him goodnight. She touched the coverlet and then opened the chest of drawers. There were many of his clothes still there. She picked up the small garments and it was then that the anger began. Whatever she had done in the past, Asterly had had no right to rob her of her child. It was an act of savage cruelty and she struck the tallboy with a clenched fist.

The earl and his wife probably wouldn't enjoy a scene which would disturb the pleasant tranquillity of their lives, but they were going to get one nevertheless.

"You bastard, Nicholas," she said aloud and hit the wood again. "I'll get Robert back if I have to kill you to do it."

Asterly was reading his post without enthusiasm. Nothing seemed to hold his interest nowadays. He felt as if he were an empty vessel with neither heart nor soul to maintain it, surviving one day after another in a kind of limbo.

When he was with Robert, some semblance of his former

self came back for a while. He loved the child deeply, but even Robert couldn't repair the harm which had been done. Only one person could do that, but she was shut out of his life for good.

He held a letter in his hand, but the words ran together and made no sense to him. Emerald wouldn't give Robert up without a struggle and he had told her servants where he was going to take the boy. She would come to Cornwall soon; it was inevitable.

The thought of seeing her again, even screaming her fury at him, made something inside him smoulder again. Ashes he thought long dead were igniting and warming him to an emotion he didn't want to feel.

He forced himself to look at the letter again, to take his mind off Emerald. It was from a friend of his, Lady Keswick. He waded through her verbose account of her tour of the shops in Paris, only a fragment of his attention on her ramblings about current scandals and the people she had met.

Then a phrase caught his eye and he sat upright, reading the paragraph again.

' ...and, of course,' Lady Keswick had written, 'the Comte de Grancey found the most exciting woman in Paris; he always does. I saw her with him one night and have to admit she was striking. She had the greenest eyes I've ever seen and hair black as night. Marcel has spent a fortune on her – jewels, furs and such like – and, naturally, took her home with him. She has that awful woman Virginie Feuillet in tow. I bribed Mme Feuillet's servant to tell me about the girl. It seems she's just come over from England and that she's called Emerald. Surely that can't be her real name?'

Asterly lay back in his chair and closed his eyes. How ruthless fate was, planting gossiping Bessie Keswick down in the French capital at precisely the same time as Emerald had been there, and with the notoriously amorous de Grancey. He could feel himself shaking with fury again. No longer dead inside, nor moved by the stirring of embers left from the past, but blazingly angry because Emerald had left their son to go to Paris to sleep with Marcel Giradin.

At one point he had been foolish enough to consider allowing Emerald to see Robert when she arrived at Cloverley Park. That was over; she wouldn't see him then, or at any other time. He got up, kicking his chair away, and went to the big house to see his father.

"It's tittle-tattle," said Radfield when he had read Lady Keswick's letter. "I know Bessie and so do you. If there's nothing going on to entertain her, she invents something."

"Are you defending my wife?" Asterly was white round the mouth. "Christ, sir, what more evidence do you need?"

"This isn't evidence. The viscountess could simply have been dining with de Grancey. How could Bessie possibly have known whether the comte took your wife home or not?"

"The viscountess? You've lost some of your sting, Father. You wouldn't acknowledge her as such when I first brought her here."

The earl considered his son meditatively. Nicholas was still locked in his prison; nothing had changed. If he had stopped caring he wouldn't have minded how many lovers his wife took, in Paris or anywhere else.

"I'm not quite sure what else to call her and you know why I've lost my sting."

"Call her what she is; a trull."

"Lower your voice, if you please. Robert might hear you. You realise she'll come soon, don't you? I imagine she's on her way by now. I don't want the child upset by your quarrels."

"Then give your servants orders not to admit her."

"Very well, but I don't think she'll give up that easily."

"Then let her seek me out and I'll make her give up."

"Nicholas, I know how you feel ..."

"So you said before, my lord, but you don't; you can't. It's one thing for you to maintain that you'd go on loving Mother whatever she did, but you know she'd never look at another man. You can't really appreciate what it's like to know that your wife will give herself to anyone who takes her fancy."

"I'm not entirely without imagination, but you're still in love with her, of that I'm very sure. You admitted it last time we talked."

The lines engraved round the corners of Asterly's mouth were harder than ever, his expression ugly.

"So I did, but I'm not so sure that's true any more. I think this *affaire* with de Grancey has put paid to that. In future I shan't love; just hate. I shall be free of her."

"First, you don't know that she's had an *affaire*, and secondly you're no more free of her than you were before. You'll never be free. In God's name, when are you going to realise that?"

"Sometimes I wish I had the courage to do away with myself."

"Don't be childish and stop feeling sorry for yourself."

The viscount ground his teeth, but he knew he would get no sympathy from his father.

"I want to see Robert."

"No."

"What do you mean, no? He's my son."

"And my grandson. You're in no fit state to see him now. I won't let you damage him because you're a numskull."

"You talk as if you think I should clasp my wife to my bosom and tell her that all is forgiven; that she can hop into another man's bed whenever the mood is upon her; that ..."

"Be quiet!" The earl's tone brooked no argument. "I'm saying nothing of the kind and please remember you were the one who married her, not I. I will not have this house set on its ear because you can't control yourself. Go back to the Dower House and shout there, if you must. And, Nicholas, when your wife arrives, remember one thing."

Asterly was seething but he knew he dared not treat the earl to another outburst.

"Yes, my lord, what would you have me remember?"

"You have said many times since you returned here with Robert that he is your son. What I want you to bear in mind before you start clawing at your wife with those spiteful talons of yours is that she is his mother and you took him away from her. Think how she must be feeling now."

"I don't care a damn how she feels," returned Asterly waspishly and made for the door. "And don't forget to tell your servants to keep her out. You said you didn't want the air in here polluted. If you still feel the same, tell Chatworth to kick her down the front steps."

Radfield looked at the door after it had slammed to with considerable force. Then he sighed.

"Poor Nicholas, you really are a fool, aren't you, and what a thing it is to be in love. Ah, Juliet, my dear. Where is Robert?"

"Norah is just bringing him down. Was that Nicholas?"

"Of course. Who else slams doors like he does?"

Radfield had had a long talk with his wife some time before and she was not a woman to blind herself to the truth. Besides, if the presence of Robert had mellowed the earl, it had done equally remarkable things to her. Her cool smile had become a beam; fine silks and satins had been abandoned for muslins and cottons which were better able to withstand the ravages of her grandson's small, sticky hands.

"I wish we could help him, Selwyn. I feel we were partly to blame because we received her as we did."

Radfield shook his head.

"That made no real difference in the long run. It wasn't what we did which broke Asterly's heart. Don't upset yourself, he'll work it out in the end."

"Do you really think so?"

He smiled at her, patting her cheek which was still as soft as the petal of a rose.

"Yes, my sweet, I do. Now give me a kiss before Robert

gets here. I might not have time for such nonsense once he arrives."

"This is another chance for you to say 'I told you so'," Emerald gave Ryan a smile devoid of humour. "You said he'd be like steel underneath the charm, didn't you? I should have listened."

Eugene had come round to Court Street as soon as one of Emerald's servants arrived with the news that she was home. He could see the fear in her and shared it. Asterly wouldn't give up easily, if at all.

"You mustn't hope for too much," he warned. "Don't expect him simply to hand Robert over because you ask him to."

"First I'll ask, then I'll demand. I'm going to get my son away from Nicholas if it's the last thing I do. He's robbed me of so much; he's not going to take Robert, too."

But when Emerald finally reached her destination and looked up at the great house standing in its fine gardens, she felt helpless and alone.

Nicholas had so much on his side. An old, proud name; an honourable reputation; parents to support him and fight for what he wanted. He also had Robert.

She alighted from the carriage, adjusting the folds of her skirt, not because she wanted to look her best but through habit. When Chatworth refused to admit her, she lost her temper completely. So many tangled feelings mixed up inside her, boiling like the cauldron in her father's cottage had done. She had expected to see Nicholas; instead she was being shut out by a servant.

She stood and looked at the closed door, shaking with rage. Then out of the corner of her eye she caught sight of someone hurrying towards her. The maid was young, cap awry, hands red from scrubbing. She bobbed to Emerald and kept her voice low.

"Shouldn't be 'ere reelly, ma'm, but I'd 'eard as 'ow you

weren't to be let in. All the servants 'ave been talkin' about it, but I don't think it's right."

"I see." Emerald's lips tightened. "So now my husband takes the staff into his confidence, does he?"

"No, no, your ladyship, it weren't like that; it were the earl's orders. What I came to say is that the boy's 'ere, but the viscount ain't. 'E's in the Dower House."

The words were chilling ones and not nice to think about. Emerald started to thank the maid, but the girl was flying back to the side entrance, her mission accomplished.

Emerald rang the bell of the Dower House four times, but nothing happened. Then she ran a few steps back from the front door, picked up a heavy stone and hurled it through the nearest window. Another followed and a second window broke into smithereens. She was reaching for a third missile when the door opened and Asterly came striding over to her.

Neither of them had expected their meeting to be so completely and utterly shattering. Hate and recriminations had buoyed them up whilst they were apart; brooding and cursing was easy from a distance.

But they were no longer at a distance. They were standing close together, sharing the same silence they'd shared many times before, looking into each other's eyes. It was as if they had seen each other only yesterday.

"I won't let you come into my house." The viscount knew he had to speak harshly and with rancour, or else he would take her in his arms and kiss her until his pride had melted away. "The stables are good enough for you. Follow me."

She had intended to dispute everything he said but she found herself obeying him, trembling because she had so nearly gone down on her knees in supplication, not asking for pity but for love.

The grooms and stableboys were sent packing and the viscount said frigidly:

"Well, what do you want?"

Emerald was herself again. The dangerous moment had passed and his rudeness and obvious distaste for her presence brought her to her senses.

"I want my son," she snapped. "What did you imagine I wanted, you?"

"Hardly. You won't get me anyway and you're certainly not going to have Robert."

"He belongs to me. You had no right to take him."

"I had every right. I'm his father, only you omitted to inform me of the fact when he was born."

"You said you never wanted to see me again. Why should I come running to you about a matter which doesn't concern you?"

"He's my heir, you damned harpy! I should have been told and you know it. Anyway, it doesn't matter now. He's where he belongs."

"He's here at the moment, but I'm taking him back to London with me."

"No, you're not." His eyes were so icy that Emerald felt frozen by them, but she wasn't going to let Nicholas see that. "He will remain here for good. You are not a fit mother. Not a single soul would uphold your case against mine. You went abroad and left him alone."

"He wasn't alone; don't be so ridiculous. He was well cared for until you came and stole him. I'd only gone to Paris for a short while."

His hateful smile made the world darken for her. Asterly hadn't finished yet, and it was the mention of Paris which made him look like a tiger about to devour its prey.

"Yes, of course, Paris. And how did you enjoy being in Marcel Giradin's bed?"

He saw her recoil and pressed home his advantage.

"Oh, yes, my dear, I know what you were doing over there. Lady Keswick, a friend of mine, saw you one night. She described you very accurately and, because she's a busybody, she made it her business to find out a few things about you. You can't help yourself, can you? You must have some doting man in front of whom you can flaunt yourself. The comte is well known for his generosity to his many mistresses and that must have been an added pleasure. You love money so much, don't you? You sell your body for it, without a second thought. Money and possessions; they're all you care for.''

"It ... it isn't true." She was stunned by the extent of his knowledge. She had no more chance of making him believe that de Grancey hadn't touched her than she had had in getting him to accept the fact that Noah Penrose had raped her. "I swear to God we were not lovers.''

"I was told he bought many things for you. Are you saying that is untrue?''

She crimsoned.

"No. He did give me gifts.''

"And asked nothing in return?'' The white teeth shewed briefly and ferociously. "What sort of cretin do you take me for? Men like de Grancey don't shower women of your sort with presents unless they are sure of repayment. And I'm sure you repaid him well; you've had so much practice.''

"Nicholas, please listen to me.''

"No! I won't listen to you, not for another minute. You wanted to be famous; you are. You wanted to be rich, no matter what price you had to pay. Now you've got money, so go and spend it, but never come back here.'' His searing fury quietened to something much worse as he dealt the *coup de grâce*. "If you do return, and make any attempt either to see my son or to take him from my care, I shall tell him exactly what you are as soon as he's old enough to understand what the dirty words mean. Is that clear to you, madam, or would you like me to repeat it?''

Emerald was reduced to silence, her colour washed away as quickly as it had come. Asterly's implaccable contempt was raining down on her, and he had won. Not for a second did she doubt that he would do · hat he promised. He would stoop to anything to get his own way and destroy her, as Eugene had once said he would.

She didn't say any more, for there were no words left which would be of use to her. He had crippled her with a single blow and there was nothing else to do but to walk back to the carriage.

Asterly waited in the stables for five minutes, making sure she had gone before he returned to the Dower House where men were already beginning to repair the damage done by the stones.

He went up to his room and sat on the bed. Then and only then did the full and devastating effect of her beauty, her magical presence and her sexuality hit home with the force of a bullet which made him shake.

He could have taken another course. He could have ignored Bessie Keswick's letter; accepted Em's word that she and Giradin had not made love; forgiven her for what she had done in the past and, in return, sought her pardon for his own sins.

Instead, he had struck her with a warning so lethal that she could never again risk coming near him. He had turned her away and lost her for good.

"Well," said Radfield after dinner, when Juliet had left the room, "and after she'd broken two of your windows, I presume you allowed her access to the Dower House."

"No, I said the stables were good enough for her and that's where I took her."

"Very hospitable. And then?"

The viscount gave his father a black look.

"Then she asked ...no demanded ...that I return Robert to her."

"And naturally you refused."

"Certainly." Asterly's attention returned to his glass. "I made her accept the fact that she'd seen the last of him."

"Really?" The earl's voice was very soft. "I should be most interested to know how you did that. I thought she'd do battle for him like a wildcat."

Nicholas didn't answer and Radfield's tone grew cooler.

"I see. I take it you won't tell me what methods you used because you're ashamed to do so."

"I'm not in the least ashamed." Asterly rapped the words out. "If you must know, I said that if she tried to see Robert, or get him back, I would tell him what manner of woman she was when he was old enough to understand."

"I knew you wouldn't fight fairly."

"Why should I? She has never done so. I taxed her with her *affaire* with de Grancey."

"Did she deny it?"

"Yes. She admitted accepting his gifts, but insisted they weren't lovers. She was lying, of course."

"Why should she lie?"

"My lord, are you serious?"

"Perfectly." Radfield poured more port, passing the decanter to his son. "She said she was Feverell's mistress and you and I condemned her for it and drove her away from here. What has she got to lose by admitting she slept with Marcel Giradin, if she had?"

"Well, because of the boy."

"But you'd already judged her unfit to look after him because of Feverell. You didn't know about the comte when you took Robert from Court Street."

For the first time there was doubt in the viscount.

"Do you think it's possible? I mean, do you really believe she wasn't Giradin's mistress?"

"Yes, I do believe her denial. Also, I've thought for a long time now that her story about the man in the cowshed when she was young was true. I think the only time she fell from grace was with Jehu Feverell, and she made no attempt to hide it."

Nicholas shifted uneasily. His father was a sceptical man, not easily taken in.

"It makes no odds," he said, trying to get rid of the maggot nibbling away in his mind. "She played the whore with Feverell. Anyway, Robert has me and loving grandparents."

"When you were his age you had me, and loving grandparents too, but when you were upset or unwell or frightened it was Juliet you wanted."

Asterly no longer evaded the earl's gaze.

"Robert is happy here, isn't he?"

"Most of the time."

"When isn't he happy? He seems all right to me."

"Yes, but you don't put him to bed. Juliet and I do that, and each night we have to listen to him crying for his mother. We don't enjoy it. He's only two years old, you know."

"Oh God!" Nicholas felt as if someone had struck a blow over his heart. "He'll forget her in time, won't he?"

"In the light of what happened today, I sincerely hope so, for his sake."

After a long pause Asterly said dully:

"I need to go away and think. I'll go to Ireland and buy some horses. You don't mind, do you?"

"Provided you don't take the boy with you. You're not going to make a nomad of him."

"Damn it, sir, he is my son."

"And when you're ready to behave like a responsible father, your mother and I will step aside gracefully. Meanwhile, if you go, you go alone."

"Oh that was a terrible thing for Nicholas to say," said the countess when the earl had told her the whole story. "I know the girl was very wrong not to have told him about herself and Robert, but losing her baby is punishment enough for anything she's done. She didn't need such a threat into the bargain. If I'd been her, I'd have ignored what Asterly said. If someone had tried to take him away from me when he was two years old, I'd have scratched their eyes out."

"Ah, yes, but no one could have told Nicholas at some later date that you were a harlot, could they? But don't worry. I know more about hitting below the belt than Asterly does; I've been doing it a good deal longer than he has."

"Selwyn, what have you been up to? What did you say to him?"

"I told him that Robert cried for his mother every night. I thought for a moment he was going to faint. His colour was decidedly sickly." The earl smiled and put his arm round his wife. "Then he said he had to get away to think. He claims he's going to Ireland to buy bloodstock, but I don't believe he'll go near a horse, do you?"

"No, but you are naughty to tell such lies. Robert never cries. Do you think ...?"

He laughed gently and kissed her.

"Yes, beloved, I think he's beginning to crack. One more push and we may be there. Meanwhile, let's forget our son's marital problems and consider our own."

Juliet put her arms round his neck, her eyes full of wicked invitation.

"Have we got any marital problems, darling?"

"I'm not sure. Let's go to bed and I'll let you know in the morning. Come on, you Jezebel, don't keep me waiting all night."

TEN

Back in London, Emerald threw herself into work like one possessed. Hour after hour she laboured over her latest designs, cutting out most of the gowns herself, spending evenings and most of the nights sewing seams which an apprentice could have done just as easily.

Verity remonstrated with her, full of concern as she watched her mistress grow thinner and wan. Only the green eyes burned as brightly as ever, but even they had a feverish look about them.

"It's one o'clock, madam," said Verity as she entered the workroom, lamp in hand. "You must stop now and come home."

Emerald looked up from the skirt she was embroidering.

"Verity? You startled me. What are you doing here?"

"I've come to fetch you and I won't take no for an answer. You can't go on like this; it'll be the end of you. Here, let me take this. You can finish it tomorrow. I'll make us a cup of tea and then we'll get back to Court Street."

Over the cups, Emerald said defensively:

"We're doing very well. Our profit's well up on last year."

"I'm not surprised, seeing the way you keep at it."

"More people come to me now; important people, I mean."

"I know."

"There's even a rumour that Her Majesty might ask me

to make something for her. That would be wonderful, wouldn't it?"

"A great honour, of course."

Emerald stopped pretending and put her cup back on its saucer.

"Yes, you're right."

"About what?"

"The things you haven't said. The money, the fame, the duchesses, the baronesses; they don't count for much, do they?"

"They meant a lot to you once."

"Not any more. I can see now which things are important and which aren't. Trouble is, this is all I've got left."

"You're missing Master Robert. That's why you're driving yourself like this."

Emerald began to tidy the reels of silk and the needles, her hands not given the chance to shake.

"Yes, of course I do. He was ... is ... so sweet. When he used to hold his arms out to me I felt warm inside; when he smiled, I wanted to cry."

"Oh, my dear."

"But it isn't only Robert. I should never have gone to Cornwall myself. I should have sent someone else to try to get my baby back. Seeing Nicholas again has made it so much worse. He was as hard and unforgiving as ever but I couldn't hate him, however much I tried. That's why I burn the midnight oil. I don't want to go to sleep because when I do I dream about him."

Emerald carried on for a few more weeks. Then she went to talk to Ryan.

"You must be mad," he said incredulously. "Sell up now, when you've got to the very top? You're the most sought-after dressmaker in London. You've worked so hard for it, too. And the house and the other things; why do you have to get rid of them as well? Em, you can't do it."

"I have to, it's the only way. If I used a hundred thousand words Nicholas would never believe me. He thinks I'm a wanton who cares only for success and money and will stop at nothing to get both. I've got to make him see he's wrong."

"But why? For heaven's sake, why?"

She gave him a sad smile.

"Because I love him. Even if I never see him again, he'll know that I was speaking the truth when I write and tell him what I've done. Will you buy my half of the business?"

"Of course, but ..."

"Verity is to have the house in Court Street. I want you to ask the lawyers to set aside a sum which will provide her with a generous income. I'd be grateful if you would see to the sale of my personal things; clothes, jewels and other items. I've put on one side every single thing the Comte de Grancey gave me. Please see that they're sent back to him. As for the rest of the money, that's to be held in trust for Robert. As soon as you can let me have the cheque I'll send it to Asterly with my note."

"Asterly's a wealthy man. He can provide for the boy."

"Robert is my son, too. I have a right to help. Nicholas won't let me near him, so this is the only way I can do it."

"But what if this absurd gesture means nothing to him? He could still simply shrug you off as a fool."

"I expect he will, but he won't be able to ignore the truth any longer. Giving up everything and going back into service again will shew him I meant what I said."

Ryan gave a quick exclamation.

"Going back into service? What are you talking about?"

"I've found myself a position as a lady's maid. I shall be working for a Mrs Aylmer who lives in Finchley. I'll give you the address but no one else is to know where I am, not even Verity. The only time you are to get in touch with me is if you hear that anything has happened to Robert."

"A lady's maid!" Eugene caught her wrist. "Em, this is utter madness. You have a great gift; you can't throw it away."

"The gift is worthless. So is everything else without Nicholas. You will help me, won't you?"

He was still aghast, but he could see that he hadn't made the slightest dent in her.

"I'll have to, but I hope you know what you're doing to me."

"I do and I'm sorry. I'm so fond of you and I'll miss you, but that's part of the penance."

"Penance!" He snorted. "Christ, if anyone should be doing penance it's Asterly."

"No, that isn't so. He may have done some bad things too but it was because of me that he did them. I shouldn't have become his mistress or his wife. I did him a terrible wrong, Eugene, and I deserved what I got. I ought to have told him about Robert, too. I do love him so and I've got to show him that by what I do."

"This is going to break Verity's heart. Have you thought about that?"

"Of course I have. This isn't a sudden impulse; I've been thinking about it ever since I got back from Cornwall."

"I still say you're wrong. The bloody man will probably laugh and tear your letter up."

"Perhaps, but somehow I don't think so. Before I ruined his life, Nicholas Roman was a fine person. I'm praying that some small part of what he once was is left."

Explaining things to Verity Dean was even harder.

"Don't do it," she cried, her arms reaching out for Emerald. "Oh, my dear, don't do it, I beg you."

"I have to, for the reasons I've just given you. You'll be all right here. I've seen to it that you'll be comfortably off."

"Do you think I care about myself? I don't want anything."

Emerald sighed, holding Verity's hands tightly.

"No, love, you didn't even want my penny, did you? Still,

whether you like it or not, you're going to be nice and snug."

"What if the viscount doesn't understand?"

"That's what Eugene asked, more or less. He'll never want to see me again and maybe his anger will never die, but he'll understand about me getting rid of my possessions and going out to work again. I know he will." Gently, she withdrew her fingers. "Go now, Verity, I've got to write to Nicholas. When Eugene sends the cheque round, put it with the letter and send it off for me. It's the last thing I shall ask of you, but it's very important."

Emerald found the letter much harder to write than she had expected. She repeated what she had said about Penrose's attack and her refusal to sleep with the Comte de Grancey. She expressed contrition about Feverell and the concealment of her past, explaining as best she could her reasons for giving everything up.

'It is to show you how little they mean to me,' she wrote. 'I've made myself two black gowns, two white aprons and some caps, just as I did when I went to Rowett Lodge. I'm starting all over again. I am going back to where I began but this time I shall take a different path and try to redeem myself, if I can. Everyone deserves a second chance, don't they, even me?

'I have made this letter too long already, but I want you to know one more thing. I loved you from the first moment I saw you. I will go on loving you for the rest of my life. If you won't believe anything else, Nicholas, please believe that. My dearest, I beg you to believe that.'

On the following Monday Emerald presented herself to Mrs Aylmer, neat and tidy, but with shadows under her eyes.

"Yes, you'll do, Tregellan, I'm sure. I'm not a fussy woman, but I expect hard work from you and no callers."

"There won't be anyone to call, madam."

Emerald looked down at the carpet in case Mrs Aylmer should notice that her eyes had grown over-bright.

"Well, that's good. Now, did I understand you to say you are able to do a bit of plain sewing?"

It was Madame Virot who raised her head, chin well up as she replied.

"Indeed I am. Plain or fancy, it's all the same to me."

And while her new mistress nodded her satisfaction, Emerald said silently and with a heavy heart:

"Sewing's like loving. Once you know how, you never forget."

Emerald's letter was waiting for Asterly when he returned from Ireland. He read it through twice and then went to find his father. The earl took one look at his son's face and got out of his chair in a hurry.

"Nicholas, what is it? Are you ill?"

"I suppose I am, in a way."

"Here, come and sit down. Tell me what's happened."

Silently Asterly handed the letter to his father, waiting as the earl read it carefully.

"What a very brave young woman," said Radfield when he had finished. "I wish more than ever that I hadn't spoken to her as I did. She had such a hard start in life, yet in spite of that she got herself to the top of her profession. We were born on feather beds; we didn't need ambitions nor did we need to work. We have more money than we know what to do with, but she had nothing."

"I know." The viscount was still numb. "The day I found out about her – when I realised what she'd done – I called her vile and filthy names, accusing her of going to any lengths to get money. She told me then that I didn't know what I was talking about. That I'd never gone to bed hungry or walked over sharp stones in bare feet, but I didn't listen. Instead, I beat her."

The earl was very gentle, for he could see Nicholas was in hell.

"You believe her now?" he asked. "She has made her point clearly enough, hasn't she? She's stripped herself of everything she possessed in order to convince you that she loves you and that your reading of her character was wrong."

"Yes, I know she's telling the truth, only it's too late."

"Why?"

Asterly's eyes were blind and without hope.

"Well, she's not going to take me back is she, not after all the harm I've done her. In any event, I don't know where she is."

"She says here that a man called Ryan is the only one who knows her whereabouts and he's promised not to divulge the information unless he hears that something is wrong with Robert."

"Then there is no way that I can find her."

"Good God, Asterly, what's the matter with you? Go to this man Ryan, who appears to have been your wife's business partner, and get him to tell you."

"How can I make him do that?"

"If necessary go down on your knees and beg. I've watched you dying a little each day; so has your mother. We can't endure the suffering any longer. You're as much in love with Em as she is with you. Why don't you do something about it?"

A flicker of a smile touched the viscount's lips.

"That's the first time you've used her name."

"But it won't be the last, if you're half the man I take you for. Be off with you. I'll say goodbye to your mother and Robert for you. You go and find your wife."

The interview between Ryan and the viscount was a long one. Eugene thought Asterly looked like a man recovering from a long illness, but he didn't let that weaken his resolve. He had given Em a promise and he intended to keep it.

"Dear God," said the viscount finally, "have you no compassion in you?"

"Did you have any for her?"

The viscount shook his head.

"No, I didn't. No pity, no understanding, no forgiveness, no mercy. I even suggested to my father that if she called at Cloverley Park he should give his servants orders to kick her down the steps. When she came to see me at the Dower House, I wouldn't let her in. I said the stables were good enough for her and that's where we talked. That is the kind of man I am."

Eugene picked up his pen and tapped it against the inkwell.

"Em said that was the kind of man she'd made you. She didn't blame you; she blamed herself."

"I can believe it, for she has in her all the warmth and generosity of spirit which I lack. But if I could die for her I would. You have the means to determine how the rest of our lives are to be spent. You can condemn us to perpetual misery, for she will be as unhappy as I am all the while we remain apart, or you can help us to rebuild our world."

Ryan looked at the viscount again. A promise was a promise, but a life was a life, too. Asterly was right: apart they would spend each day in purgatory.

"You'll find her here," he said, scribbling the address on a piece of paper. "It may not be easy, my lord."

"I know, but nothing worth having is ever easy to obtain. You have my heartfelt thanks and don't worry about Em any more. She'll be safe in my hands this time."

Emerald put on her chip bonnet, black cotton gloves, and a shawl which she drew over her shoulders.

It was her free afternoon. Four hours of being by herself with only her thoughts to keep her company. The Aylmer household was a noisy one, but Emerald didn't mind that. While the children were chattering and laughing she could listen to them instead of remembering things best forgotten.

It was true that one of the boys, much of an age with Robert, sometimes made her want to cry when she looked at him, but she steeled herself to get on with the job she had chosen for herself.

She had made up her mind not to let anyone know that she could do more than conjure up an apron or two from a length of cotton, but somehow her fingers had betrayed her. Mrs Aylmer was delighted with the dresses which her new maid produced and in the end Emerald was glad to be back doing what she knew best. There was some small satisfaction to be gained from it and Oonagh wouldn't have wanted her to waste all that tuition.

She let herself out of the servants' entrance, a small demure figure making for the Common. No one looked at her as she started to cross the grass. If she closed her eyes she could pretend she was on the clifftop at Porthaven again, lying full length and watching the village below. She didn't have to imagine what lords and ladies were like any more; she knew. It seemed to spoil the game, but she thought perhaps she was getting too old for such childish fantasies.

As she opened her eyes and went on walking she saw a figure in the distance, but it was a long way off. Just another Finchley dweller out for a stroll, taking the air.

When she grew closer and saw who it was her heart plummeted. Eugene would never have told Nicholas where she was unless he knew Robert needed help.

She ran towards Asterly in panic.

"My lord! It's Robert, isn't it? Is he ill or has there been an accident? He's not ... not ... dead, is he?"

"God, I'm a clumsy idiot." Nicholas caught her hands, feeling her dreadful trembling. "No, no, it's nothing like that. The boy is in the rudest health; he's with my parents. Please, please don't look like that."

She shut her eyes again, waiting for the giddiness to pass.

"I'm all right now," she said unsteadily. "You don't have to hold me any longer, I'm not going to faint."

"I'm sorry; truly sorry. I just didn't think. I should have realised that seeing me like this would have such an effect on you."

"It doesn't matter." She still kept her head lowered, not

wanting him to see what she was feeling. "Why did you come?"

"It's not easy to explain. Shall we walk on for a while?"

"If you wish."

"You're very pale; thinner too."

She gave him a sidelong glance, unable to resist the temptation. His apology had been quick and genuine; his voice was free of venom and so were his eyes. He looked just as he had done before her world had been torn apart.

"I work hard. It's good for me."

"Not if it makes you look as you do now."

When she didn't reply he said hesitantly:

"I came to answer your letter."

"No answer was required. How did you know where I was?"

"Ryan gave me the address. A maid at the house said you'd probably be here on the Common."

"Eugene wouldn't have done that. He promised never to let anyone know, and even he was only to get in touch with me if there was anything wrong with Robert. That's why ..."

"I know, I know. I had no intention of frightening you, I swear it. Ryan didn't want to tell me and I had to beg."

"Beg?" She felt a flicker of new life run through her, trying to check it because in spite of what he was saying he still had the power to hurt her in so many ways. "That isn't like you, my lord, and I really do not see why you are here. We have nothing to talk about. I set it all out in my letter."

"You may have said everything you wanted to; I've said nothing so far."

She stopped and turned to him.

"Haven't you? I would have thought there wasn't much you could add to our last conversation."

It was as if she had hit him and suddenly she wanted to comfort him and tell him not to be so sad, but she kept her hands by her sides and her mouth shut.

"I asked for that, but you said everyone was entitled to a

second chance. Don't I qualify for one, too?"

"What would you do with your second chance, my lord?"

"Don't keep calling me that. You make it sound as if we are strangers."

"Aren't we?"

"No, you're my wife."

"A fact which you still find abhorrent, no doubt."

He caught her by the shoulders and shook her hard.

"Stop it, Em; for God's sake, stop it! I know I deserve it, but we've wasted enough time."

Even his rough handling was pure bliss and she was glad that he kept hold of her. He could still stir her to excitement as quickly as he had ever done.

"All right." She was almost meek. "What is it you really want to say?"

She was praying hard, sorry when he let her go.

"I'm not sure where to start; perhaps with your letter. I do believe you. I didn't before, as you know well enough, but when I learnt what you'd done; that you'd given up everything you'd ever struggled for, for my sake. I knew my father was right."

"The earl believed me?"

He saw her amazement and gave a rueful grin.

"Yes, he's a good deal wiser than I am and he is quite changed. He's sorry for what he said to you that morning; as sorry as I am for what I said and did. The day after you'd gone, he told me he'd looked at my mother on the previous night and realised that even if she were a proven ..."

"Whore, harlot, strumpet; take your pick."

He frowned, unhappy again.

"Yes, if she were, it wouldn't matter to him. He knew it would not stop him from loving her. He said I hadn't stopped loving you either. I admitted that much, but I was too proud, stubborn and stupid to do anything about it. I nursed my anger and my hurt pride and when I saw Robert it burst into fresh flames. I should never have taken him; it

was a wicked thing to have done. Then I heard from that
wretched Keswick woman about the Comte de Grancey
and it was the last straw. I didn't stop to think; I just froze.

"When you came to see me at the Dower House, all my
torment, misery and jealousy crystallised into a weapon
which I used on you with a barbarous inhumanity."

"Don't make me out to be too innocent." Emerald knew
the most important moment in her life was approaching
and it frightened her. "I really did intend to sleep with
him."

"So you said, but you couldn't do it in the end because of
me. Em, how can you go on loving me after all I've done to
you? That's the only part of the letter I find hard to
accept."

She gave a half-smile, still fearful in case she was in one of
her childhood daydreams and Nicholas wasn't really there
at all.

"That's the truest bit of all. As I said, I loved you from
the first day I saw you. Nothing will ever alter that."

She waited for him to choose his words, holding her
breath.

"I'm thinking of buying a house in Cornwall." He gave
her the kind of hopeful look which Robert did when he
wanted something special. "It'll have to be fairly near to
Cloverley Park because my parents couldn't bear it if they
didn't see Robert every day. If I can find a suitable
property, do you think you might come and throw stones
through the windows now and then?"

Her eyes filled with tears.

"You wouldn't mind if I did?"

"No, but I'd rather you came back and lived with me."

"Don't say that unless you really mean it, Nicholas. I
couldn't bear to have such happiness snatched away
again."

"I mean it."

"Would your father object?"

"He sent me to find you. I would have come anyway, of

course, but he just gave me a push. He said he couldn't go on watching me die a bit more each day and that was what I was doing without you. Oh, my dearest, dearest Em; I love you. I love you!"

The next second they were in each other's arms, blinding joy and blessed peace mingling together as their lips met.

"I wouldn't mind the Dower House," she said after a while, holding on to him so that he couldn't run away. "It's very conveniently placed."

He frowned at once.

"I would mind. My shame is locked up in one of its rooms."

"Then open the windows and let it blow away. It's over and done with. Robert will soon be old enough to walk across the garden by himself to see his grandparents. We may sometimes have other things to do, don't you think?"

His smile caressed her, his arm tightening round her waist.

"I know we will. Are you quite sure you don't mind going back there? After what I did ..."

She put her fingers over his mouth to silence him.

"I'm certain. I'd live there, or anywhere else, as long as you were with me."

"I shall be there, sweetheart."

Their second kiss lasted a long time, for it contained passion, regret and an awareness of a new beginning. When he released her, he undid the strings of her bonnet, casting it aside. Then he took the pins from her hair so that it tumbled down to her shoulders in shining disarray. For a moment or two the dark tendrils swirled in the wind, curling back against her cheeks which were already showing the colour of her exultation.

He studied her in wonderment, thanking God for giving her back to him. She was his wild girl standing by his carriage; looking up at him from the fence at Rowett Lodge; sitting on the grass in the copse; playing the grand lady in her fashion house; lying in bed with him, her body close to his. She was the mother of his child.

He said very softly:

"You are the most beautiful woman I have ever seen, or ever hope to see. You are also the most seductive, tantalising and alluring little baggage I know. Come on, Emily Tregellan; let's go home."

They called him the Gypsy—and Lady Campion had to trust him with her love and her life!

From the tranquil kingdom of her country house in England to the bloody heart of Revolutionary France, the beautiful, spirited Lady Campion is drawn into a deadly trap—and the bait is the one man she cannot resist.

The Fallen Angels

Susannah Kells

——90192-5 $3.95 U.S.

"Outstanding—I loved it!" —Johanna Lindsey

"Exhilarating" —United Press International

"Spellbinding" —*Booklist*